Emma Comes Home

Ann Baker

Copyright © 2020 Ann Baker

All rights reserved, including the right to reproduce this book, or portions thereof in any form. No part of this text may be reproduced, transmitted, downloaded, decompiled, reverse engineered, or stored, in any form or introduced into any information storage and retrieval system, in any form or by any means, whether electronic or mechanical without the express written permission of the author.

This is a work of fiction. Names and characters are the product of the author's imagination and any resemblance to actual persons, living or dead, is entirely coincidental.

The views expressed in this work are solely those of the author and do not necessarily reflect the views of the publisher, and the publisher hereby disclaims any responsibility for them.

ISBN: 9798577094621

PublishNation
www.publishnation.co.uk

TO RWB AND PJB, WITH LOVE.

EMMA COMES HOME

Emma Hird got off the bus, two stops before home, just as she had done for the past ten years. By walking the last two stops she saved 10p. Times 5 days, and reversing the process every morning she saved one pound each week, this she kept at the office out of prying eyes.

She walked slowly through the dark and the cold rain, there was no rush to enter the house she called home. She looked at it as she approached the gate and regarded the place objectively.

Broken gate, peeling paintwork, dim interior lighting, curtains and nets which had hung there the whole of her 26 years. How had it come to this? She was literally a prisoner, bound by duty to the mother whose poverty she had grown up with. The mother who had scraped together every penny to keep herself and three children in food and charity shop outfits.

Her father had left when she was 12, unable to take any more of her mother's constant demands for more money.

She still remembered the rows. Her father shouting that it was immaterial how much he earned, she still made it disappear. What did she do with it? It certainly didn't go on good food, warm rooms or home comforts. If she needed more she would have to go out to work herself, and see how she would like it! In the end he simply left, walking away with one small suitcase, the three children watching his figure growing smaller as he walked down the road. They never saw or heard from him again.

Her mother had not shed a tear, she had simply called them together and told the boys, then 14 and 16, they must go out and find a job. Saturday work, paper rounds, leaflet drops. Anything which would help them to make ends meet, and of course the money would have to be handed over each week. This they dutifully did for two years, getting up at dawn to mark and deliver papers before school.

The first battle began when Robert her eldest brother announced he wanted to go on to university and study architecture. His grades were excellent, and gained him a good place, but he needed help with accommodation, books, travel. The answer, swift and hard, was no. With no father she expected him to take a job locally and make a large portion of his wages over to her. She had kept and fed them for years, now she demanded some return for her sacrifices.

Robert had simply said he was going to university come what may, and at the end of the summer term went to live with a school friend, whilst holding down three different jobs a day. Somehow he paid his way, buying second hand books, sleeping on mates floors and going hungry. Waiting at tables in the restaurant meant he got at least one meal a day, weekends he helped steward at local sports events and holidays he took any full time work he could find. Eventually the university had seen his struggle and found him a room at the top of the main building. It was literally no bigger than a broom cupboard, but he had free rent, light and heat, a futon to sleep on and somewhere quiet to study.

With a 2.1 degree, he got his first job as a junior architect in a well respected London firm, and never came home again.

Alan her second sibling was an easier target. Leaving school at sixteen he got himself apprenticed to a motor mechanic and spent every spare moment tinkering with old cars and learning how to repair them. He dutifully tipped up his wages and was grudgingly given just enough money to see him through the week. The trouble began when at 18 his boss gave him an old banger and encouraged him to see if he could put it back on the road. Working weekends in his own time he got the car roadworthy and sold it, buying another wreck with the cash. Three cars later he had made enough to pay for his lessons and got his driving licence first time.

He may not have had Robert's brains, but he had clever hands, he told Emma.

The buying and repairing of older cars, providing you found the right vehicle was making him some extra income, this he steadfastly refused to give his mother, though she demanded it as her right. He had learned from the other garage lads that no one ever turned their wages over to the extent he did.

After one particularly awful row he had confided in his boss at work. The older man did not want to lose this budding mechanic who could make engines practically talk and suggested he went to look at some flats which were being created from the old Co-op building in the town. They were well planned, partially furnished with fitted kitchens and wardrobes, ideal for a firsttime buyer, and with references and payslips he got his first mortgage. He was on the property ladder.

Emma was sorry to lose an ally, but he came most Sundays, took her out and taught her to drive. 'Not that I shall ever own a car' she told him. Now old enough to leave school, she had taken a job at the local Solicitors and was in the Conveyancing Dept. Mother claimed losing Alan's wages meant they could barely manage and she handed over most of her wages each week.

She was now almost 26, and, she told herself she had spent ten years in this routine. The short walk from the bus stop did not balance out her sitting down job, she was thickening round the waist and her second hand clothes and sensible charity shop shoes, never quite in fashion made her look like the beginnings of spinsterhood.

Standing in the rain at the gate, her thoughts and memories had brought her full circle. How did she break out of this situation without leaving her mother to abject poverty. They were already living on just her salary and the council tax, electric, water and gas bills for the large rambling house were huge.

With a shrug, she pushed open the broken gate and found her door key. The rain was running down her face, her hair dripping. The first three complaints would be, 'You're wet, you're late and don't drip on the floor' she thought.

The house was cold and quiet. By now, teatime in autumn, Mother lit the fire and they had a small amount of heat until the cold forced them to bed, only one shovel of coal per night was allowed. Hanging up her wet coat and changing her shoes for shabby slippers she walked towards the kitchen hoping just for once there might be something reasonably tasty for dinner. Her pack-up sandwiches, eaten at 1.00pm were only a memory, she was hungry.

CHAPTER TWO

Pushing open the door she stopped and looked down in horror.

Her mother was laid full length on the kitchen floor, the old broken bladed potato knife still in one hand. She was the colour of pale candles, waxy and very still. And very dead, Emma thought. She had never seen anyone dead before, but she knew this is how they must look, as though something inside them had been switched off.

Kneeling down to touch her, Emma found she was icy cold, this had happened some time ago, she was sure.

'I stood outside', she was thinking, 'I stood outside wondering if this situation would ever resolve, and it has, she's dead.' She felt totally and utterly calm, this woman who had dominated their lives, taken every penny she could from them, made the boys get up and work before and after school and had not had a holiday since her husband had walked out, was finally gone.

Going next door to borrow the phone, she told her neighbour Mrs Jenks of her discovery and received a cup of sweet tea in return. By the time she had drunk it, the paramedic had arrived, Alan, her brother was on his way and Robert had promised to travel up in the morning.

The sympathetic police officer who arrived, explained all sudden deaths had to go to the mortuary. It was arranged quickly, the officer kept her talking, distracting her, whilst two gentlemen in black overcoats and a dark van, coming quietly into the kitchen and wrapping her mother, carried her gently away.

Alan arrived looking pale and shocked, Emma told him Robert would be here the next day and they would have to make some arrangements. Neither of them knew where to even start.

Mrs Jenks, always a kindly woman, had been rebuffed and discouraged by their mother from being too neighbourly for years, but the children had loved her and had received many a secret treat, a bar of chocolate or even a cinema trip on the quiet. Now she was a tower of strength, explaining how the system worked and suggesting a local funeral director.

'There is nothing more we can do tonight,' she said, 'unless there are relations, cousins, friends who need to know?'

They both shook their heads, there really were very few people who would care, their mothers meanness had seen to that.

Later that night when Alan had gone home, she was tucked up in Mrs Jenks' spare room. Emma couldn't help but marvel at the difference between identical spare rooms in identical houses. This room had pretty curtains, a soft carpet, lovely white cotton sheets and more importantly, it was warm. It could not have been any more different to her own room next door, with its thin polyester bedding, old eiderdown and a bed she knew to be almost as old as she was. What a difference having money made, she thought.

Next morning she rang work, and broke the news to her boss. Mr Ainley, who was Senior Partner at the solicitors had long since recognised her worth as the best conveyancer he had ever had, and after giving his commiserations told her to take as much time as she needed. As he pointed out, she never took her full holiday entitlement anyway.

Alan and Robert both arrived just as Mrs Jenks was putting a good breakfast on the table and she made all three of them sit down and eat. She waited until they had finished eating, then looking slightly flustered she joined them at the table for a second cup of tea and listened to their conversation.

Robert always the practical one, wanted to know how much a funeral was these days. Alan said however much it was he was sure they couldn't afford it. And Emma said nothing, she could see her savings disappearing into her mother's funeral. Surely all that walking in all weathers wouldn't be for nothing after all.

'Can I give you a bit of advice?' Mrs Jenks said, rather timidly Emma thought. 'When you go through your mother's papers make sure you find everything, you know, bank and building society books, things like that.'

The three siblings looked at her in total astonishment, mother had nothing, which was why they had struggled all these years.

Mrs Jenks looked rather embarrassed, 'I think you'll find you may be mistaken, and there is money you may not be aware of.'

Robert looked at her curiously, 'How do you know?'

The woman flushed, looking even more uncomfortable, 'I can't say, it might get people into trouble, but my Harry's niece has a sister in law who works at the building society, and perhaps she's said more than she should.'

'Well, Robert said, 'If we find only one pass-book it might help with the funeral, shall we start our search kids?'

CHAPTER THREE

The house felt even colder than usual when they entered. Alan got the fire lit and burning brightly with plenty of coal, and Robert managed to fire up the central heating boiler. As it was only switched on in the coldest of weathers it was a miracle it still worked at all, Emma thought.

They agreed they needed to start their search in Mother's room, it had always been her private sanctuary and even as children they had been discouraged from entering without her permission. The large first floor bedroom gave the appearance of being just as poor as Emma's own. The old double bed with its sagging mattress took up one end of the room and the only other furniture was a large wardrobe and a strange looking piece of dark oak which Emma had once been told was a 'marriage'. For years when she was young, she had believed this must have been a wedding present but had since realised a 'marriage' simply meant two pieces of furniture placed together, one on top of the other, which hadn't originally belonged to each other.

It was Alan who made the first discovery, the bottom of the wardrobe had a drawer fitted in its base, and the top of this provided a shelf for shoes. He had removed the old shoes and taken out the drawer which had contained a selection of old hats. Under the drawer was the floor of the wardrobe, but his mechanics mind saw that the dimensions didn't tally and with a little prodding he found there was a wooden slider, it moved sideways and revealed a shallow cavity, its depth half hidden by the wardrobes bulbous legs. It was full of brown paper bags, the sort you got from the greengrocer, folded and made into small parcels they filled the hidden space.
    'Bingo.' He called as he carried the parcels across to the bed, there were seventeen of them.

They gathered round as he undid the first parcel, snapping the old rubber band around it. What appeared next stunned all of them. Twenty pound notes, had been neatly stacked into an oblong and wrapped in their brown paper coat and fastened with the rubber band. Alan counted them out, there was one thousand pounds. There were seventeen packages.

It was Robert, who spoke first. 'The bitch, the miserly old bitch, I slept on floors, I worked three jobs, I actually went hungry, all because she claimed she had nothing to help me through Uni. How could she, when all along there was money hidden here in her room?'

Emma was one step ahead of them, 'This isn't passbooks or bank accounts, there must be more, Mrs Jenks niece's sister in law, or whoever, couldn't have known about these.'

They continued their search, Alan went out and brought in sandwiches at lunchtime, and it was almost three o'clock before they found the real treasure trove. The ugly piece Mother had always called a 'marriage' appeared to have several secret drawers and compartments, taking out a small drawer, and pushing her smaller hands to the back of its space, she had heard a click and the back had opened. She pulled out a wad of papers and several envelopes, calling 'Geronimo!' to bring her brothers running.

Here were the building society and bank pass books going back years and years. Many were full, the balance having been transferred to the next book and so on. She must have been squirrelling money away all their lives.

Emma sorted the different banks into three piles, then taking the most recent book from each pile opened them slowly. The last entries were two years old, but roughly adding up the final entries from all three books, she looked down at the figure and literally sat down on the bed with a crash.

The three books totalled almost £400,000, some of the early entries going back 30 years and there would be interest to be added for the last two years, she calculated.

Putting her head in her hands, she simply wept, the tears streaming unchecked down her face. Not for her mother, but for herself and the two boys. This was unforgivable, her lost opportunities, the missed social occasions when she had refused any invitation because she had nothing to wear that was even remotely like a party dress, a lack of boyfriends and above all her missed teenage years when she could have learned to jive and skate and enjoy her youth.

Her brothers looked on helplessly, neither used to seeing a woman in so much distress,

'Go make some tea.' Robert said to Alan, 'we are going to have to take this slowly.'

Later, when they had all calmed down and were sitting round the fire, they pieced together what had happened. Mother had stopped going out shopping and into town just over two years ago, finding the shops and public transport beyond her. That was when she must have started hiding the money at home, all the building society and bank book entries ceased at this time.

Robert had found one more hiding place by moving a piece of the elaborate carving and found a stack of envelopes. These had caused the three of them more distress than everything else put together. They were addressed to their mother and in their father's handwriting, looking at the dates, they had arrived at monthly intervals for years and years. They could only guess what they had contained, but Robert with his analytical mind, voiced their thoughts. Their decent father had sent her money for years, she had told no-one and kept it, when she knew it had been meant to be shared and to pay towards his children.

She had continued to allow them to believe that he had never been heard of again, never written or sent a card, and had coloured their opinion of him as a deserter and an uncaring father for years.

CHAPTER FOUR

They were still sitting in the growing darkness when Mrs Jenks came round to say the Coroner's office had rung, the post-mortem would be tomorrow and if everything was satisfactory they could have the body by the day after. Looking at their faces, she said gently, 'Would you like me to ring the undertaker and ask him to call? He will be able to deal with all that side of the arrangements.'

'Yes, please,' said Emma, suddenly glad to be able to make some firm arrangements. 'I'm going to pack a bag, the three of us are going out for a decent meal and we are spending the night in the Travel Lodge.'

In the end, Emma agreed it wasn't the best idea with all the money they had found still in the house, so they ordered a magnificent Indian Banquet takeaway, had it delivered and ate until they were stuffed. After which Alan went home, she returned to Mrs Jenks and Robert slept in her old room.

As they could do nothing until after the post-mortem, it was agreed Robert would bank the money next morning, using his own savings account. Emma's job was to talk to her boss, Mr Ainley, about the lack of a will and Alan would get a days' work in, which would keep his boss happy.

She took her usual route to work, but today she stood at the bus stop opposite her home, it was a small act of defiance, no more walking two stops to save 10p.

Bob Ainley was pleased to see her and invited her into his office when she asked if they could talk. Without giving him too many details she told him about their discovery, her mother's hoarding and the things they were unable to find. The will, if there was one, was missing, and her pension book. Emma couldn't imagine she had missed out on collecting that, the day it became due.

'Its good news and bad news' he said. 'The good news is I have a copy of her will. When she approached me ten years ago and asked if there was a job for you here, I pressured her into making a will. It was almost a trade-off, she needed a job for her daughter and I wanted the business.

We'll get it up from the strong room for you, but it's perfectly straight-forward, the three children inherit everything. The house of course, is paid for, so that will fetch a tidy sum in the current market.'

Emma was stunned, sell the house? Of course, why not? She didn't want it, cold, rambling, shabby, it needed an energetic young couple with D.I.Y. skills. She could have a flat, or an apartment, she could live anywhere she wanted.

'Don't worry about her pension,' her boss said, 'that will be paid directly into her bank, so if you haven't found it, there's a bank account somewhere.'

Bob Ainley went on to say he would make a phone call to a friend who ran an antique shop in town, 'he's honest, not like some of them. I'm going to ask him to come and look at this 'marriage' of yours, experience tells me they usually have far more secret compartments than the one or two you have found.'

As she was leaving his office, a thought suddenly struck her, 'you said the good news and the bad news,' she queried.

He suddenly looked embarrassed, 'I shouldn't have mentioned it now, not when you are coping with your mother's death. But the rest of the staff have been informed so you were bound to hear of it. I have sold the practice, I'm sixty-five this year, and I got an offer from Willows that I really couldn't refuse.'

Willows, thought Emma, one of the biggest chains in the country, famous for buying up and amalgamating small legal practices. Aloud she said, 'Willows, they have their own large conveyancing department, don't they?'

He nodded sadly, 'I'm sorry, my dear, they intend to amalgamate most of our work into their own departments, and that will include conveyancing.'

Emma nodded. 'So, I've lost my job and my mother in the same week!'

He looked so miserable, Emma hadn't the heart to say any more, but left to collect her mother's will from the strong room, with his assurances that the redundancy money would be generous, ringing in her ears.

On her way home she paused to look in the brightly lit shop windows, something she hadn't done for years. Yes, she thought, job or no job, I can certainly afford a few new clothes.

The next few days were a blur, the friendly calm undertaker made all the necessary arrangements, moving her mother from the mortuary to his premises and booking a slot at the local crematorium. All three siblings agreed there would be no church service, just a simple commitment. 'At least she would have approved of us spending as little as humanly possible' Alan had said with a grin.

CHAPTER FIVE

On the day of the funeral they were surprised to find more people than they had expected. Several attended from both Alan and Emma's work, the Jenks came with the neighbours from the other side and Robert appeared with a pretty young woman, whom he introduced as a friend. His workplace didn't even know he had a mother, he said. Whoever was there, came for the sake of the three children, not their mother, her meanness had been too well known. There was no wake, just a simple commitment and once it was all over, people simply returned to work.

The three siblings took Mrs Jenks and her husband out for a meal as a thank you. Emma was still enjoying the comfort and warmth of their spare room, and as Alan said, without her they might have let the old furniture go without ever knowing there had been a fortune hidden inside it.

The Antique Dealer had been a triumph, finding two more cavities, the missing pension details and bank account, an out of date passport and her birth and wedding certificates. He had also pointed out that although very shabby the furniture was of extremely good quality and made them an offer for it. It would need renovating in his workshop, but he had worked that into the price.

Robert said she had inherited it from her grandparents and taken it instead of having to spend money on new.

On the evening of the funeral they had sat and faced each other. The local estate agent had reckoned they could get well over a million for the house. A ridiculous amount, it was falling to pieces! You'll get it, he assured them, there are huge gardens, it will be snapped up by a developer and he'll put at least one more house on the plot, if not two. The house is in poor condition, but the rooms are large, it has four good bedrooms and there is room for a splendid conservatory on the back.

'Why didn't she sell up and downsize years ago?' asked Emma.

The agent explained that silly as it may sound, she had done them a favour, prices were going up month on month, and it was now worth twice what it would have been just a few years ago. Commuter belt houses were in high demand, and they already had a list of people just waiting to come around and view.

He asked them, rather tentatively, if they thought they might have a skip. He felt the rooms would look even more spacious once some of the dreadful carpets, curtains and beds had gone.

Emma explained the antique items were going immediately, having been sold. As she was using up her holiday leave and had no job to go back to anyway, if Alan would give her a hand with the heavy items she would clear the house. What was useable would go down to the Charity shop, what was unsaleable would be skipped.

Alan agreed, and to their surprise Robert said he would be taking a week off work to help as well. 'If we work together, a week should do it,' he said.

Once the estate agent had left with his papers signed agreeing to handle the sale, the next hurdle was what to do with Emma. At least that was how she put it to the two brothers.

Alan said, 'Emma what do you want to do, you will have the money to do whatever you want or live wherever you wish.'

She had spent years thinking about this. Her two brothers were only thinking of the last few weeks, but Emma had dreamed for years of escaping from the net her mother had woven. She wanted some decent clothes and a holiday, a long holiday she said. A new place to live could wait, as long as she had the money, she could take a break first and then come back to find somewhere to buy.

'Right' said Robert, 'Alan and I have discussed this and we are both in agreement, mothers will states we divide the assets three ways, we don't agree.'

Emma's stomach turned over, surely they weren't going to try and cut her out?

But he went on, explaining that the money found in the wardrobe was to be hers. Only you were bringing an income into the house, Alan and I were long gone. That money is yours, we both agree on this, no arguments.'

'Treat it as a bonus, he said, 'Have the holiday you want and take your time.'

'But I have my redundancy to come,' she said weakly. The two brothers were adamant, the redundancy payment might come in useful when she came back and was looking for another position. The wardrobe money, as it was always referred to, was to be hers.

CHAPTER SIX

A month later, with the Wardrobe cash propping up her meagre savings, the house was empty and they had accepted an offer on the house for the full asking price from a local builder. Whatever he intended to do with it, Emma simply did not care.

Three weeks ago she had walked into the local Thomas Cooks, and approached the desk of a homely middle-aged lady, who had looked up and given her a warm smile. Her lapel badge said she was Linda.

Emma explained she had lost her mother, was between jobs and had decided to take advantage of the gap to take her first holiday in years. She required somewhere warm but not too hot, somewhere green not a desert location, preferably where they all spoke English and had a public transport system.

'Would you prefer them to drive on our side of the road as well,' Linda said with a grin.

Why not, thought Emma,

By the time Linda had ascertained that Emma had no passport, had never even flown, had not had a holiday since a school trip to Bruges and wanted to go for at least three months, she was on board. This was the sort of challenge she loved. 'You need amazing weather, friendly people, a relaxed environment and no wars or trouble zones,' she told Emma.

She sent her off with a pile of brochures with possible locations and instructions to have her photo taken and apply immediately for a passport.

It took three weeks and several visits to Linda, before they finally agreed on the trip, but they had become friends and Emma was sure she had found the right destination for her first adventure.

Robert had paid the wardrobe monies into her new bank account, and she passed over her debit card, another new acquisition, with a flourish. She would have three weeks in an all-inclusive hotel, this would give her time to look around, and then she would take a self-catering apartment and look after herself for a few weeks. The airline ticket would have an open return, this way she could choose to come back to the UK whenever she wanted.

When the two men asked where she was going, she almost shouted with happiness and excitement. 'Barbados!! She said, I'm going to Barbados!'

Linda spent her lunch hours in town, so at Emma's suggestion they met up for coffee and a sandwich in the local department store. She and Emma had been to the luggage department and Emma had chosen a bright blue suitcase which was on special offer with a piece of matching hand luggage. ' Don't get black,' Linda told her, 'They all look alike on the carousel.'

Over coffee, she gently asked Emma if she had thought about her wardrobe for the trip. Emma laughed ,'That was one reason I wanted to see you,' she admitted. She explained a little of her mother's lifestyle, and how there had never been money for new clothes. 'I need a decent warm coat,' Emma told her. Linda laughed, 'That's the very last thing you need in Barbados, I propose a lightweight mac!'

Linda suggested she make an appointment with the stores shopping consultant, a person who searched out the items suitable to your needs and budget. 'Sometimes,' Linda explained 'They suggest items you wouldn't have dreamed of trying on, and because they have an eye for it, they can make you look absolutely fabulous.

Emma thought about this, Linda was right, she had no idea where to start. On her way out she stopped at the Customer Relations desk and made an appointment for the following afternoon.

By next afternoon she was so nervous, she almost rang and cancelled the appointment, what would the consultant think when she saw the old-fashioned clothes and shoes which were all she had to wear. She needn't have worried, Di was big, bouncy and more than anything else, kind. Exactly what Emma needed, someone who would take her in hand and giving her the confidence to try on various outfits.

'Clothes for three months in Barbados!' She shrilled. 'Fabulous. You need cotton, preferably crease resistant and very lightweight. Let's start in the Ladies Summer Section, and we can move on from there.'

Two hours later, she was the proud owner of three pairs of lightweight slim leg trousers and a selection of tops, all of which could be mixed and matched. There was a pair of beautiful black silk evening trousers, together with two flattering shirts, one very dressy lacy dress and three swimsuits with matching cover ups. Emma had to be almost manhandled into the shorts, but Di insisted she would wear them, if she had her way Emma would have been in bikinis not swimsuits.

Trust me, she told Emma, Barbados is casual during the day, you will find eighty year-olds in bikinis and they look great.

They arranged a further appointment, Di wanted her measured correctly for bras, and new cotton underwear was a must. Shoes to travel in, trainers would be fine. Then sandals, flats for walking and heels for evening.

With only ten days to go before her flight, Emma had moved into the local Travel Lodge. The builder was anxious to get started and although Mrs Jenks had said she could live there with pleasure, Emma wanted somewhere to spread out her new purchases and try them on in her own time.

She arranged for a beautiful bouquet of flowers to be delivered to her kindly neighbour, without her they might never have begun the search for her Mother's hidden wealth.

Her second appointment with Di had brought her lovely new underwear, lacy bras, a very lightweight fine cotton dressing gown, or robe, as Di called it and some pretty cotton pyjamas.

'No nylon,' Di had cautioned, 'far too warm.' She had also picked out a couple of pretty cotton summer dresses which would be perfect for evenings in the hotel, she had said. As they acquired various items Di had produced costume jewellery and showed her how to dress up an outfit, 'Nothing valuable' she said, 'Just ring the changes and enjoy.'

At night she read the travel itinerary over and over again. Fine if you were a regular traveller, but confusing for a novice. All those instructions about not carrying liquids and putting her make up in a plastic bag. Make up! She thought, hell's teeth I need help there.

The hairdresser in the high street had been there for years, and didn't have the smart stainless steel and plastic look so many of the new establishments had. She was pleased to find it was friendly and, yes, they did sell make up and gave lessons.
The assistant was about her own age, but her makeup and hair were perfect, if only I could look like that thought Emma. She stood behind Emma's chair and studied her, examining the shape of her face, the way her hair grew and parted, her skin colouring and eyebrows.
'It's all or nothing,' thought Emma, 'I've spent a fortune on clothes and a holiday, might as well look the part. 'Be honest,' she told the girl, 'I haven't been anywhere like this before, what do I need?'

The girl took a deep breath. 'Honestly, you need a haircut, before we can even start on your face, we need to reshape your hair.' So instead of the makeup lesson she had booked, she sat and watched her dark hair falling to the floor around her. Mothers answer had been to tie it back in a rubber band, and when it got too long she simply cut some off the length. Now when she looked at the person in the mirror, it was to see a shiny sleek bob which could be turned under or over depending on the occasion. 'Buy yourself a pair of straighteners, the girl advised. It's a lovely colour, in great condition, just needed styling. A once a month trim should be fine.'
'Better not tell her I won't be here in a month,' Emma thought as she walked down the High Street feeling slightly light-headed. She had remade her appointment for the make up lesson and would be returning next day.
When the receptionist at the Travel Lodge whistled and told her she looked fabulous with her new hairstyle, it really made her day.

Emma took a great deal of pleasure in her new purchases, the hair preps. the straighteners, the new clothes and the expensive make up. She spread them out on her bed in the hotel, trying on various outfits, experimenting with the costume jewellery as Di had shown her, and getting used to seeing herself in make up.

Her first outing in new clothes had been to the office, partly to say farewell to the staff and to thank Mr. Ainley for his generous redundancy payment, but really, she told herself, deep down it had been to show them she could look just as smart and up to date as they were. The sniggers and sideways glances at her second hand clothes had hurt. This time it was compliments, and genuine pleasure at seeing her, 'You look so happy you glow,' one of the girls had said.

CHAPTER SEVEN

By the time Alan dropped her outside Departures at Gatwick she was a bag of nerves. Alan had grinned, 'You need your tickets and your passport, it's too late for anything else now, go on Sis, you'll be fine.'

He bent and gave her a brotherly kiss, the first time ever, she thought, as he handed her the big case. She turned and waved as the automatic doors opened for her, but he was already back in his car and driving away.

She hadn't told either brother, but she had actually done a dummy run last week to the Airport, finding her check-in desk number on the Departures Board and making her way towards it. She had watched other passengers checking in and discovered there was even a train going between terminals.

Now as she approached the Virgin check-in desks a man in a smart uniform asked to examine her ticket and then directed her to the red carpeted lane which announced it was World Traveller Plus. Emma hid her smile, world traveller indeed! If only they knew, she thought. However, this avoided the much longer queue next door. The friendly red-suited check-in clerk, smiled and asked for tickets and passport. She really shouldn't have spent so much time worrying, the case was well under the permitted weight, her hand luggage was given a little yellow tag, and she was done. Clutching her boarding card with its ringed items, showing her seat number and gate, she headed slowly towards security.

Again she felt her nerves taking over, have I got any liquids, will they pull my case out, will the scanner ping as I walk through. It was all for nothing, she walked through the scanner without it making a sound, her carry-on case was waiting for her at the other end of the belt and she was through.

Duty free was a revelation, she treated herself to some perfume, after trying lots of different ones. She also fell in love with a handbag which would be perfect with lightweight summer outfits and bought it. She then chose a couple of good reads from W.H.Smith, and by the time she had treated herself to a cappuccino it was time to wander down to the gate. Here they had begun loading by seat numbers and priority boarding, and she found herself going down the long corridor which led straight into the big plane.

A Virgin hostess noticed her lost look and showed her to her window seat. Putting her purchases in her carry-on case, she hoisted it up into the locker above her head and keeping her books for the journey she settled herself into the seat. There was a blanket and a small pillow, they obviously expected her to have a sleep, she thought.

The howl of the engines as it tore down the runway took her breath, how these steel giants ever got into the air with all the weight they carried, simply defeated her.

She loved the flight, her companion turned out to be an elderly Bajan lady returning home to Barbados, and she proved to be a mine of information on the island and the flight itself. Emma ate, drank, watched a film and had a nap, this was luxury. By the time they began their descent into Barbados, it was growing dark, and her companion in the next seat laughed, 'You'll soon get used to the night, it comes very quickly in the Caribbean,' she said.

'What is the purpose of your visit?', said the Immigration Officer.

'A long holiday' Emma replied, and realised for the first time that she really did mean it, she could stay as long as she wanted.

Returning her passport he smiled and said. 'Enjoy.'

A luxury hire car was waiting for her, and she was swept north, travelling up the centre of the island to avoid the coast road which was always packed at this time of the evening. They passed roundabouts all named after famous cricketers and the lights of Bridgetown, the capital, glowed on their western side. Finally the car turned downhill towards the coast, and crossing another main road they drew up in a pretty courtyard, lit by torches and a smiling doorman came to open her door.

'Welcome to Holetown' he said, My name is Raol, and this is where the very first settlers from England landed in the 17th Century.'

Her warm welcome with a cold towel and a rum punch whilst checking in, made her feel more cared for and cosseted than she had for years and years.

CHAPTER EIGHT

The four hour time difference woke her far too early, but by 7.00am she was dressed in the shorts and t-shirt Di had insisted she would need and was out of her room. Walking down three flights of steps, (promise to herself kept, no elevators,) she was transfixed. The hotel ran straight down onto the beach, the sea was only 25 yards away, and above everything else, was its colour.

Under this cloudless sky, it wasn't just turquoise blue, it was dozens of different shades of turquoise and it advanced lazily on the whitest sand she had ever seen. Throwing off her sandals she walked northwards for 20 minutes along the waters edge. There were dark rocks, covered in small crabs which scuttled away as she approached, rock pools, brain coral, pieces which looked like the bones of fingers, small fish darted about in just a few inches of water and in the shallows she glimpsed a turtle. Turning to walk back she faced the full heat of the sun and realised she had not applied any sun cream, this was the southern hemisphere, she would be bright red by lunchtime. She made a mental note, first priority a large sun hat.

Breakfast, a lounger bed, a dip in the warm sea, an aperitif at 11.30am, before a fabulous lunch, a siesta, another lounger bed, another swim, shower and dress for the evening, a pre-dinner drink in the bar and dinner. This was her routine for the next three weeks, guests arrived and departed, but everyone spoke, she joined in conversations round the bar and chairs were pushed towards her to join their groups. She learnt to laugh at the sudden sharp showers, all over within minutes and the hot sun quickly drying up everything, liquid sunshine, the Bajans called it. She also stuck to her promise to eat properly, fresh fruit at breakfast, salad at lunchtime and a sensible evening meal, already she felt her new regime was paying dividends, some of her new clothes were quite roomy.

In between times, she went sight-seeing, visited gardens full of exotic orchids, explored caves and other beaches. One Friday night they all went by mini bus to the famous Oistins Fish Market, and full of fish, black rice and local beers sang all the way home on the bus.

Her travels around the island had made Emma rethink her idea of renting a condo or an apartment. After the friendly atmosphere of the hotel she thought it might feel lonely, particularly if she was several storeys above ground. She voiced these fears to Raol, the friendly Doorman, and he looked thoughtful. 'Why don't you think about a chattel house?' he said. 'Some of them have been beautifully modernised. You can sometimes find one to rent whilst their owners are back in the UK. You would have neighbours, there are usually a few shops or stalls for food and you would be able to use any beach you wanted. Don't forget in Barbados, every beach is open to the public.'

Privately, Emma thought these houses looked rather small, but as he had offered to make some enquiries she thanked him and said it might be a solution.

To her surprise, he came looking for her a couple of days later, in his hand a slip of paper with a UK telephone number. 'My Mum gave me this he said, it's the house next door to theirs. The lady is back in the UK, her mother is very ill, and she's staying there 'till the end. If you give her a ring in Bournemouth, mum thinks she will let you rent her place for a while.'

Emma thanked him and wandered into Reception. It would be 8.00 at night in the UK, she might catch her in, and she asked reception to help her make the call.

Mrs Bristow was like a breath of fresh air, a very breezy breath. 'Go and have a look at it,' she advised. ' Two bedrooms, a bathroom, lounge and kitchenette. Parking space for two outside and a deck for sitting. If you like it, I'll ring Raol's mum and if she thinks you're suitable you can have it.'

She went on to explain to Emma that her elderly mother's illness was terminal and she would not be returning until it was

all over and the old lady's flat disposed of. 'I shall want a fair rent, and I also want one month's notice on either side, I would guess you could have it for about three months.'
'That would be perfect.' Said Emma.

Like it! Emma loved it on sight, small and cosy and of course, warm, whatever the weather, it was so different to the cold huge London house her mother had clung on to. She had expected one of the tiny chattel houses which now held chic boutiques up on the west coast! But this was much larger and more spacious. Mrs Bristow had given it an utterly modern make-over without spoiling the old exterior and it felt just right. The timbered walls were pale cream and the modern fittings and furniture didn't look the slightest bit out of place. The floors had been sanded and polished to a lovely shine, with just the odd rug to break up any areas.

Outside, the small deck faced west and Emma could see herself watching the sunset with a glass of wine in her hand. ' I'm getting quite poetical,' she thought.

She rang Bournemouth again, to say, 'Yes please, I would love to live here and the décor is perfect just right.' Mrs Bristow laughed, 'That's Sandy's work, best designer on the island.' She said.

In order to put things on an official footing she advised, Emma was to go see Toby Ogle, a young solicitor in Bridgetown. He looks after my interests, especially when I'm away, he'll draw up a small contract, collect one month's rent and a bond in advance and then you can have the key, I'll arrange for Raol's mum to let you in.

Next morning Emma wandered down Bridge Street looking for a name plate, Toby Ogle was in a slightly ramshackle upstairs office over one of the many jewellery shops. When she rang the downstairs doorbell there was a click and the old door mysteriously swung open on its hinges with no one there and gave access to a steep flight of stairs. By the time she reached the top she had solved the mystery. The cord which lifted the latch to allow her access ran up the door, along the steep staircase and into the office at the top of the stairs. Then it ran around the room until it came to rest behind the chair of the young man sitting there. All he did was pull on the cord whenever anyone rang for admittance.

'Ingenious' she said with a smile.

Toby Ogle laughed, 'Lot cheaper than a receptionist,' he said. He was a six foot two Bajan man, and should have been modelling for a men's fashion catalogue, his even features and large brown eyes made him one of the most handsome men she had ever seen.

Once she had explained her mission, he got to work and taking down her current address and details, he said. 'When have you to vacate the hotel?'

'I've one more week, I know I should have organised something before this, but I haven't had a holiday since forever, and just got myself lost in the days.'

Toby laughed, 'That's Bajan time for you.' He said.

As he began to draft a short rental agreement, he found Emma doing most of it for him, adding clauses and termination dates. His curiosity aroused, Toby put down his pen and said

'What was your occupation in the UK, Miss Hird?'

'I was Head of Conveyancing at Ainley's Solicitors, they amalgamated with Swallows and I was made redundant. My mother died the same week, so here I am having the first decent holiday of my life.' She smiled brightly, not wanting him to think she was looking for sympathy.

He simply sat and stared at her. 'My Lord, have my prayers really been answered?' he said, somewhat shakily.

'I don't understand.' Emma said.

'Miss Hird, I am a one man band. A new Solicitor trying to establish a practice on this island. Consequently I get the little jobs, when I should be concentrating on the bigger fish. Last night I actually prayed for help, I am drowning in Conveyancing, and it is not my strength. Today, you have appeared.'

'Oh, I see,' said Emma, but she didn't really, was this gorgeous black man, who was just beginning his career asking for help?

'Look, if you need some help, I understand you still follow the British legal system here, do you want me to help you catch up on a backlog?'

'Backlog, he almost barked the word. 'Miss Hird, Emma, I desperately need someone, even if it were only for a few days. I'm just no good at conveyancing, it's not my strength.'

They sat and looked at each other. In the end Emma said that if he did her rental agreement she would return the next day and look at the files.

'Could you take the phone calls as well, he asked rather shamefaced. I'm so behind, they keep ringing and demanding results.' Emma grinned, if there was one thing she was used to it was clients who wanted results.

By 8.00pm the same evening, she had the keys to her new home. She could only guess that Toby had rung Mrs Bristow, and assured her this was an excellent tenant, and she had given him the go-ahead. In return Emma promised to be there at 9.00am on Monday morning and to take a look at the back log of conveyancing files.

Back at her hotel, she was able to reassure reception that she would be moving out the following Saturday, as per her booking. She had loved this total change, experiencing care, good food, the exercise, the friends she had made, and above all the total realisation that she no longer had to return to a cold loveless house at the end of each day.

CHAPTER NINE

On Monday morning, in a pair of the straight cotton trousers and a smart shirt Di had talked her into, she walked into Toby's office. 'Where do we start?' was all she said.

He had obviously been busy all weekend, the second room had been converted into a small office, there was a new, albeit second hand desk, a comfy chair and a brand new computer winking away. On the desk was a telephone extension to Toby's in the main office, and the tiny kitchen had acquired some china beakers, milk, sugar and above everything else a Nespresso coffee machine, together with its pods.

Toby grinned when he saw her, 'I've spent next month's rent' he said.

She spent the morning on the internet, loading the files she required and setting up her e-mail. Once On-line she contacted her old office in the UK, and got them to send blank templates of the forms and files she would require, so much easier than designing her own she thought. At mid-day the phone rang, and remembering Toby's request, she answered in her brisk English voice. 'Toby Ogle Solicitors, can I help you?'

The voice was elderly and angry. 'Where's Mr.Ogle? where's my paperwork? he promised to get the conveyancing done this week.'

'This is Mr.Ogle's Conveyancing Department' she said sweetly, 'What name is it, please?'

As he gave her his details, she scrambled frantically through the two foot high pile on her desk, finally coming across Charles Brown at the bottom of the pile. A quick glance told her it was a straight forward transaction, a house purchase in St. Lucy, one of the northern parishes.

Picking up the phone, she asked, 'Could you come in tomorrow afternoon Mr.Brown, we could complete then. Just ask for Emma Hird when you arrive.

The rest of what could have been her lunch hour was spent putting the files in date order, the oldest one at the top of the pile. She then spent the rest of the day working on Mr. Brown's acquisition and was amazed when Toby pointed out it was five-thirty and time they went home.

Travelling home northwards on the local bus Emma realised that her new house would be much nearer Bridgetown and a shorter journey. Perhaps she ought to consider a little car, she thought.

Charles Brown, Toby had informed her next day, was one of the more difficult clients, he probably owned a lot more property than Toby knew about, but was elderly, could be cranky and was extremely secretive. This made dealing with him difficult, as you never got the straight answers you were looking for.

'Here he comes', he said gloomily, looking out of the window.

'Tell you what, you make yourself scarce, let me have a go at him.' Said Emma, well used to elderly conveyancing clients. Toby didn't need telling twice, he disappeared into his office in seconds.

Emma got up and headed into the kitchen and switched on the coffee machine.

When Charles Brown finally made his way up the stairs, puffing and blowing, she came towards him, her hand outstretched and wearing her sweetest smile. As she ushered him into the chair opposite her desk she said. 'I'm delighted to meet you do come and sit down. Do you want sugar in your coffee, I've just made you a cup.'

'Where have you come from, and where's Toby?' he enquired grumpily.

'London, she said brightly, 'Head of Conveyancing in our London office, bringing with me all the latest laws and technology. You'll find your properties will be handled much more speedily in future Mr. Brown, I promise you.' As she spoke she put a pen in this hand, turned around the sheaf of papers to face him, and got him to sign and complete his transaction.

'That it? He asked.

'Absolutely, said Emma. Unless you have something else you want to discuss, after all I'm paid to look after your interests.'

'Huh', was all she got, as he gathered up his papers and began to take his leave.

Toby could not believe his eyes, how did she manage that, it usually took hours to finalise his acquisitions.

Emma said the secret was to have everything absolutely ready when they arrived, that way they had nothing to complain about and no excuse to stay.

She took her leave of the hotel on Saturday morning as arranged, thanking staff who were sorry to see her go. When she arrived at her new home, she saw someone had cleaned all the windows and tidied the little garden, the place shone. The taxi man carried in her large case and departed. She stood in the cool modern lounge and looked around, for the next three months all this was hers, she could hardly believe it. Hanging up her clothes and putting the empty cases away in the spare bedroom she got out her notebook.

Food, milk, coffee, tea, fruit, cleaning products, bath oil, shampoo, soap, moisturiser, she wrote. If she was in Bridgetown working she could pick up most items in her lunch hour, but she felt it was important she got to know her immediate area as well.

She found an old packet of Earl Grey in the cupboard and made herself a cup, there was no milk or sugar. Emma took it outside and sat on her deck at the rear of the house, but soon she became aware she was being watched. Two bright eyes were watching her from the other side of the fence separating her property from that of Raol's Mum. A small girl was studying her intently. She hid her smile and said, 'Hello, My name's Emma, what's your name?'

'Lisamarie' said the voice.

'Well Lisamarie, why don't you come and sit here, then we can introduce ourselves properly?'

There was a sound of scrambling through the bushes down the side of the house and a small girl appeared. Dressed in a pair of old dungarees with a red ribbon on her curly hair, she smiled shyly at Emma.

'Come and sit down and let's introduce ourselves.'

'Mam says Mrs Bristow approves of you.' the child said.

'That's good news, you wouldn't want a bad neighbour would you?'

'Definitely not.' came the perky reply.

'Now, as we are going to be neighbours, will you help me to find out the things I need to know?'

The girl nodded eagerly.

'The first thing I need are some groceries, drinks, fruit, cleaning materials and shampoo. Where can I buy all these things Lisamarie?'

The child thought for a moment, 'You mean a big shop?' she asked.

Emma nodded, 'A really big shop.'

The girl scrambled down from her chair, 'You wait here, I'll ask Mam' she said.

Which was how Raol's Mum came to be sitting next to her and advising on various topics.

'Call me Winnie,' she had said, pleased to have a neighbour instead of an empty house, 'I won't let Lisamarie bother you, but we are pleased to have the house occupied and if you need anything, do let us know.' When Emma put the question of groceries to her, she laughed.

'There's a big supermarket just a bus ride away, I usually go on a Saturday, so today is your lucky day, come with us and get what you need.'

By early afternoon Emma found herself on a local bus with Winnie and Lisamarie heading to the shops. She was pleasantly surprised to find a shopping centre which had everything she needed. Winnie pointed her in various directions and she worked her way down her list. When she met up again with her neighbours it was to find they too were loaded down, and she had her own half a dozen large bags she could barely carry.

'Forget the bus, she told them, 'Let's jump in a cab, we can't carry this lot home on the bus.'

Winnie looked doubtful and Emma realised she had probably put the offer badly.

'I'll treat us to the cab,' she said, 'You've been so kind showing me where everything is, and I'm really grateful.'

They took the first taxi in the rank and Winnie chatted to the driver all the way home, Emma listened to their conversation but still found most of it incomprehensible, she really was going to have to concentrate on the local accent.

With the driver's help they unloaded their bags and whilst Emma settled his bill, Winnie and Lisamarie carried in the bags and stacked them on her doorstep.

'We'll not bother you, but if you want anything, just shout over the fence.' Winnie said.

Emma knew over the next few days there would be more items to add to a list, but for now she had food for a few days and much needed toiletries and fresh milk. One of these cartons she immediately put into the freezer, so she need never be out of milk again.

She cooked herself one of the chicken breasts she had bought, putting the others in the freezer and made a crisp salad. Then taking one of her afternoon purchases, a glass of wine, she went back to the deck and watched the most amazing sunset, and a sky which had turned every colour from red, to orange to pink, before the suddenness of the dark.

Emma suddenly realised she was absolutely shattered, took a quick shower and turned in. The bed was amazingly comfortable, good old Mrs Bristow, she murmured as she fell asleep.

CHAPTER TEN

On Sunday morning she watched Lisamarie and Winnie go off dressed in their Sunday best, and guessed they were going to church. Wearing her swimsuit under her dress and a pair of comfy sandals she packed a towel, sunscreen, hat, book and a small amount of cash and set off to find the beach. She walked for 30 minutes and was rewarded when the coast came into view, a narrow beach of white sand, with a view of the port in the distance.

Here she hired a sunbed from the shack selling beers and ordered an early lunch of blackened fish which was delicious.

The afternoon was spent watching the boats, including one of the enormous liners which called regularly at Bridgetown. When they disgorged as many as 3,000 passengers into the town, it was preferable to be out of reach she thought. The beach was busy, families spending their day off with children or friends, but once again Emma felt no sense of isolation as she had in London where nobody spoke. Here the Bajan friendliness was all around her and everyone spoke or smiled.

She enjoyed a long swim and then to her surprise a nap. Which meant she was dry enough to put her dress back on for the walk home. It had been a simply lovely day, she thought as she climbed once more into Mrs Bristows magnificent bed.

A week later, working her way through the conveyancing backlog she took a phone call from Charles Brown, he was selling a property, could she fit him in this afternoon?

'That's progress' said Toby, He asked! Usually just turns up without an appointment.'

By the time the old man had struggled up the stairs she had his coffee ready together with a ginger biscuit, and got him to sit and get his breath back.

She chatted about her recent house move, her friendly neighbours and her walk to the beach for a Sunday swim, until she thought he had the breath to talk. He was selling one of his rental properties which had become vacant. When Emma looked at the price, she paused. If she were ever to stay on in Barbados, perhaps one day she could find something similar.

'Right, Mr B. Give me three or four days and I'll have this sewn-up for you, I promise.' she said, with her brightest smile.

As he rose to leave, Charles Brown lent forward and dropped something on her desk.

Emma looked down. It was a toffee wrapped in its little twist of paper.

She thanked him and said she hoped it wasn't the sort of toffee that pulled your fillings out.

For the first time he smiled. 'Do what I do,' he said, 'take your teeth out first.' And at that he disappeared down the stairs.

She was still laughing when Toby came in to see how the meeting had gone.

That night Toby took her out to dinner. He was almost pathetically grateful for her input. It allowed him to get on with more serious cases and these in turn meant time spent in court, and absences from the office.

They drove north, almost to the top of the island and he introduced Emma to his club. Here there was a modern beautiful harbour, a squash and sports club, a good gym, pools, bars and restaurants. Toby said being a club member didn't come cheap, but brought him into contact with builders, bankers, hotel owners, and all the other trades who often needed a solicitor. They ate in the club restaurant and afterwards joined several others in the bar, where she was introduced and made welcome.

A beautiful dark girl came to sit beside her and asked if she was the girl who was renting Mrs Bristow's house. When Emma admitted she was, she explained she had been responsible for the modernising and decorations.

'You must be Sandy, Mrs Bristow told me about you', Emma told her, 'and she was singing your praises, she's right, the house is lovely.'

They stayed late, they were a nice crowd and although much of the talk was local gossip about people she didn't know, they included her in their conversations and made her feel really welcome.

When Toby finally dropped her off outside her new home, she thanked him for a lovely evening, and he simply said, 'Emma, the thanks should be all mine, I don't think I could have survived much longer without you.'

Two weeks later Toby walked into her little office and said. 'Emma, what are you doing for Christmas Day? Have you made any arrangements?'

She looked at him in astonishment, Christmas? She hadn't given it a thought, without the cold and wet, the dark mornings and miserable weather, it simply hadn't dawned on her how near it actually was. She thought back to all those previous holidays. No Christmas cards, little in the way of gifts and a very begrudged chicken dinner. It had never been a time of excitement, laughter and joy, she had grown to dread the whole holiday and couldn't wait to be back at work.

'Honestly Toby,' she said, 'I hadn't realised it was so near, it never meant much at home.'

Toby laughed, 'That's exactly how lots of us felt, so three years ago we started Christmas for Singles. It's people like us with their families in the USA and UK or anywhere abroad, or even folk who are widowed or single. We take over the Club and get together and have a real family Christmas, but with our friends instead of absent relations. It's always a sell-out, but Sandy has moved mountains and got you a ticket, please say you'll come.'

Emma was speechless, of course she would love to come, a real Christmas, for the first time ever.

How do you explain to someone that you have never had a tree, a pile of presents, fairy lights, a turkey and a house full of warmth and laughter.

A week later, with a manicure, a pedicure, hair trimmed, make up perfect and dressed in the lace dress Di had assured her she would wear one day, she was picked up in the minibus which was already full of excited guests.

The Club caught her breath, beautifully decorated, thanks to Sandy's input, she guessed. The theme was silver throughout, highlighted with a deep rich purple, an unusual choice, but it worked.

The bar was serving champagne cocktails or Bucks Fizz, and she listened as the noise level rose. The barman, a long serving employee, called it his 'Chatterer.' It certainly worked, Emma thought.

They moved into the dining room, circular tables seating ten, white linen, purple candles and napkins, table centres of exotic Bajan flowers and a gift on each plate, beautifully gift wrapped and labelled with the name of each guest.

She unwrapped her gift slowly, it seemed a shame to spoil the lovely ribbon and paper. The Jo Malone perfume thrilled her, she had never owned or even smelt such luxury.

The food was superb, five courses with their appropriate wines. Nothing was rushed, and everyone had a chance to get to know their fellow diners. Further down the room was a table of older guests, probably widows or singles, these were people who would normally be spending Christmas Day alone, and amongst them she spotted Charles Brown. He seemed to be deep in conversation with a slightly younger man, and the pair of them were looking at her. She had to smile, they were an extremely lively lot, making quite as much noise as the younger crowd.

There were no speeches, just the Club President wishing everyone a wonderful day.

By the time the tables were cleared, the sounds coming from the ballroom told them the orchestra had arrived, and the dancing was about to begin. Emma was thankful her old school had insisted on dancing as part of the curriculum and was soon on the dance floor with the rest of Toby's crowd.

It was the best night of her life, her dress was just right, the music perfect and she had no shortage of partners. It was the sort of thing she had dreamt about for years, laid in her old bed in a cold house, she had never believed it could happen to her.

As the evening finally began to wind down and the Last Waltz struck up, she had just enough champagne inside her to walk calmly across the room and holding out her hand, say to the elderly man sitting alone watching the dancing, 'Mr Brown, will you have the last dance with me?'

'Emma, my dear, you look lovely.' he said, as he rose and took her in his arms.

He was surprisingly light on his feet, had obviously danced for years, and was flattered to be asked.

'You're making all the older matrons very jealous,' he told her.

'And you can stop pretending you're short of breath when you climb our stairs.'

He laughed. 'We're dancing on the flat, it's the steps I don't like,' he said, as he escorted her back to her table.

The man who had been sitting watching them, suddenly laughed. 'He beat me to it, I was just going to ask you myself,' was all he said.

The minibus heading south dropped her off at her gate, the inebriated crowd had sung all the way home, and she had joined in. She ached, not with the cold or damp, but from dancing and laughing.

It had been without doubt the best Christmas of her life. Hugging her gift of Jo Malone perfume, she waved until they were out of sight, then turned and let herself in to Mrs Bristow's lovely home.

Next morning she got up late, and taking her hangover with her, walked to the beach. A long swim, lunch, and an even longer nap than usual and she was back to her normal self.

As she let herself into the house, her phone was ringing. It was Sandy with an unexpected proposal.

'Tried to catch you last night,' she said. 'Toby tells me you're closing the office until New Year.'

It was true, he hadn't had a holiday in years, and since they were up to date, thanks mainly to Emma, he was having a complete week off. When she had asked him what he intended to do with himself, he had replied he intended to stay in bed for most of it!

'If you have the week off Emma, why don't you come with me? I'm going to Miami to meet my regular clients there, there's a flight in the morning, if you can amuse yourself whilst I'm working, we can then get some shopping and sightseeing in.'

Emma didn't hesitate, most of the clothes she had brought from England were now too large, and although Winnie had taken them in where possible, this was the perfect opportunity to replenish her wardrobe. She needed more swimwear and was desperate for shorts. The thought made her laugh, to think she had had to be bullied into buying just one pair.

'If I won't be in your way, I would love to come.' she told Sandy.

'Right, give me your passport details, I'll book the flight for you, and pick you up in the morning, is 8 o'clock OK? Oh, and do bring a large suitcase, if we're going to do some shopping, there's no point in just a carry-on.'

The airport was busy as usual, but soon she was sitting next to Sandy as they left the island behind and settled down for the four hour flight. A drink, lunch, and an opportunity to get to know each other's history.

Sandy explained she had gone to college in the States and done her apprenticeship in Miami. She knew the city well and loved its smaller shops and smart boutiques, 'We could visit them all!' she said enthusiastically. She told Emma her father was dead, but her mother still lived in St.Lucy one of the northern parishes and famous for the longevity of its occupants.

In return Emma told her a little of her own background. She had two brothers, Robert an architect and Alan a car mechanic, both her parents were gone. She had been made redundant at the time of her mother's death and after selling their house, had decided on a long holiday or even a complete change of lifestyle.

While Emma dozed, Sandy puzzled over this information. She felt it was only half the story. This girl was bright, Toby had reported her conveyancing skills were brilliant, but in other ways she appeared very hesitant, even naïve. This was only her second flight, she had obviously not travelled or holidayed abroad, which was unusual in a girl of twenty-six with a decent job and salary. Sandy had noticed her reluctance to make decisions on simple things such as a menu or wine list, almost as though she was unused to them. At the same time her clothes and shoes were new and good quality, (Sandy had simply no idea that Emma had taken every second-hand stitch of clothing she possessed and dumped the lot.)

Whatever had happened to Emma didn't matter to Sandy, the two girls had become immediate friends and she liked her enormously, not only for the help she had given to Toby. One day she might confide in me, she thought, settling down for the last hour of their flight.

The hotel where Sandy always stayed greeted them warmly, the doorman expressing pleasure at seeing her again. This was a very different place to the Travel Lodge she had used before leaving the U.K. and much larger than the small friendly holiday hotel in Holetown. It was very grand and palatial, with sweeping staircases and banks of lifts. A reception desk which appeared to go on for miles, and restaurants, cafes, bars and coffee shops everywhere. Their room held two huge queen size beds, the bath looked big enough to swim in, and there was even a phone in the loo, she told Sandy, as she excitedly explored the suite. Sandy, quite used to this, just laughed at her delighted exploring. Her client would be charged for their stay, and the room rate would cover them both.

For the next three days she sunbathed and explored whilst Sandy met and advised clients. During the evenings they shopped and then sank into comfortable restaurant seats surrounded by their bags. Emma had a much better idea now of what suited her and the climate. With Sandy's encouragement she had finally bought a bikini and matching wrap, also several stylish outfits which she would never have tried on without Sandy's flair for finding just the right thing.

She treated herself to a fabulous raincoat, lightweight but waterproof. That was her only concession to bad weather she thought. She had a haircut, taking another inch off her bob, which had grown surprising quickly, Sandy said it was the warm weather which made both nails and hair grow. The stylist had also added a few highlights which gave her chestnut brown hair a lift.

By the time the taxi took them back to the airport, she could see the sense of the virtually empty case she had come out with. It was now full of lovely new clothes. Back on the ground in Barbados, Sandy went through immigration with her Bajan passport, joining the shorter queue for residents. Emma had to join an enormous crowd of holiday makers who had just arrived from the U.K.

The immigration officer's computer showed she had entered Barbados in November, and here she was back again.

'Are you still on holiday, Miss Hird?' he asked.

'Yes, I've been to Miami for a few days, but now I'm back.'

'Where are you staying?'

'I'm renting a chattel house, whilst the owner is abroad, it is only a temporary arrangement.'

He returned her passport and nodded her through, where she found Sandy waiting for her in the Arrivals Hall.

CHAPTER ELEVEN

The taxi had deposited her and a heavy suitcase full of new clothes outside Mrs Bristow's, she felt exhausted, and let herself in with a sigh of relief. This was short lived, Winnie must have been watching out for her return, and knocked on her door.

'Sorry to bother you Emma, but there's been a gentleman looking for you, said would I tell you he needs to see you straight away.'

'What sort of gentleman, I don't know many.' Emma asked.

'Elderly, short, bossy, and he had the biggest car I have ever seen, said his name was Charles Brown.'

Emma flopped down in one of the elegant chairs. It had come to something when clients start calling at your home, she thought. How did he know where she lived, and a large car? Didn't even know he had a vehicle. She decided he probably wanted some urgent conveyancing, well, he can damn well wait until we reopen on the 2nd January, she decided. She certainly wasn't going to open the office before then.

She had eaten so well over the last four days, she simply made herself a cup of Earl Grey and after a quick shower, retired to bed and slept a full eight hours. Next morning, feeling excited at the thought of all the goodies inside it, she hoisted her case onto the bed and began to unpack.

That was when there came a banging at her front door.

She might have guessed, only Charles Brown would think he had the right to invade her days off. 'Mr Brown, the practice is closed until January 2nd, you have no business that won't keep until then, and certainly not to call here at my home.' she began, as he brushed past her into the room.

'Emma, he said, 'I've been trying to get hold of you since Christmas, it's not about my properties, it's about you. Do you remember the chap with the white hair I was talking to at the Dinner?'

Emma nodded, wondering where this was leading, and suddenly realising that the old man was really quite distressed.

'It's all my fault really,' he went on. 'I was telling him about Toby's new Conveyancing Department, how you'd come from England to set it up and how efficient you were.'

'That was very kind of you, but I don't see…..'

'His name is Frank Freeman, and he's in charge of immigration and employment applications, and he said he would have remembered yours, it's a specialist subject, Emma, you haven't got a work permit, have you?'

Emma's stomach dropped, her throat went dry and she looked at him in horror.

'I didn't know I needed one, it started as a favour to help Toby out and I never gave it a thought,' she said.

'Well, Toby must have known, he's a Bajan Solicitor, for God's sake, of course he knew. It's against the law and you can't just walk in and fill a vacancy, it has to be well advertised and offered to a local if they can show they are qualified to do the job.'

Suddenly Emma could see her new life, new friends and this lovely island disintegrating before her eyes. Would they deport her, or even worse put her in prison? How could Toby have ignored this?

Charles Brown looked at her face and knew she was telling the truth, she had simply had no idea there were regulations she should have followed.

His face softened, 'Emma, get hold of Toby, we'll meet at the office tomorrow and see what we can do. I haven't lived here nearly seventy years without being owed a few favours.'

Once he had gone, she went back into the bedroom and looked miserably at the pile of new clothes. All the joy had gone out of them, if she was deported, she would never have the chance to wear half of them. Bikinis and shorts didn't really work in London during January.

She then rang Toby and told him of her visitor. There was a long silence at the other end of the line, which was far more telling than a protest of innocence.

'Emma, I'm so sorry, I have been meaning to do it, but it meant you making a decision on whether you wanted to stay or leave, and you were so good I couldn't face losing you, and I was so afraid you might choose to return home.'

'We're to meet Mr Brown at the office in the morning, I don't know what, if anything he has in mind, but we need any help we can get, I don't want to be deported!'

They talked for another ten minutes but the conversation was only going around in circles, Emma more frightened than angry and Toby pouring out his apologies.

Emma knew she had made a huge difference to the success of his new practice. By taking conveyancing and will-making off his hands, she had left him with time to develop more lucrative cases, and the practice was just beginning to benefit and see the difference. In return she was experiencing a tremendous job satisfaction, seeing it begin to prosper.

Toby picked her up next morning on the way into the office. She had a sleepless night behind her and her stomach felt as though it held a skipping rope. She'd had the foresight to bring fresh milk with her, feeling they might well need coffee to sustain them.

By the time Charles Brown came puffing up the stairs Toby had got out any papers he could find regarding immigration and employment and spread them across his desk.

While Emma made coffee, Charles gave Toby the dressing down of his life. 'Thoughtless. A cavalier attitude towards the law. Utterly irresponsible. Endangering other people's aspirations and livelihood.' These were just some of the comments she remembered, the whole episode seemed to go on a long time.

In the end, she turned from the tiny kitchen, put a cup of coffee in front of the old man and said 'Enough, it is my fault just as much as it is Toby's, I should have looked into it before I took the job. If there is no way round it, I shall simply have to leave.'

'It won't come to that,' said Charles Brown. Privately he thought he might have gone a bit over the top frightening them both. But he could not have allowed the situation to continue, the longer it had gone on, the more trouble it would have caused.

'I've spoken to Frank, and explained you had been here simply helping out a friend with a huge backlog. This has been so successful you now need a Short Term Permit, that will give you eleven months work, we need to apply for this straight away if you want to continue working. '

'Would it help if we explained I had not been paid for my services?' Emma said.

This was true, she hadn't needed money immediately, and when she had realised Toby really was just starting out as a Solicitor, she had suggested she wait until they were established. Once they began to make money, Toby would begin to pay her a salary and she would then receive a bonus for her past services.

Charles looked at her sharply, if this was true and could be proved, she hadn't really been employed, simply helping out a friend.

'You'll need to fill in an application for a Short Term Permit, I'll get one, and you can pick it up from my place. I'm not trailing down here again.' This was his last remark, as he stomped down the stairs,

reaching the street door, he turned and said, 'You'll owe me, big time, after this!' With that, he was gone.

'He's right, said Emma, 'We need to go for the eleven month application, the Long Term is far more complicated.'

Later she left the office feeling much better about the whole mess, at least now they were doing something, and she felt confident she could rely on Charles Brown. The one advantage they had was his ability to take it to the Immigration Officer directly, not wonder if it was spending hours sitting on someone's desk, unread. CB, as she had begun to call him, had said he was going to the Club that evening, and was sure Frank would be there.

Toby dropped her off at home and as it was still only early afternoon she gathered her towel and gear together and took her usual route to the beach.

The following morning, taking his address from his Conveyancing file, she borrowed Toby's car and headed north to Charles Brown's home. She almost missed the hidden sign, but driving up hill through fields of sugar cane she came to an old stone gateway and turning in caught her breath in amazement.

In front of her was a lovely old Georgian house. Unlike most 18th Century Barbadian houses which had one or even two flights of steps leading up to the first floor, this was all laid out at ground level. The wide veranda ran across the front, with four Doric columns, two each side of an arched door with a lovely old fanlight. Emma parked just inside the stone entrance and walked slowly up a gravel drive with a garden of exotic flowers and greenery bordering each side of the path. There were three long windows to each side of the door, each hooded with shutters to keep out the sun, and above them a portico to help with shade, upstairs was another row of seven smaller windows, once again with hoods over the window tops. Emma thought it made the windows look as though they were winking.

Years of conveyancing had given her some knowledge of periods, and she knew this to be late Georgian. It felt neat and tidy, even the trees shading the front were trimmed and looked well behaved. She guessed it had been modernised and improved, but its title 'Carroll Great House', told her it had been a slave plantation once.

The housekeeper directed her round to the back of the house, where she found Charles sitting in the shade with a jug of something which looked cool and refreshing in front of him. He rose when he saw her, poured her a glass and smiled as she settled in a comfortable padded chair.

'A Great House, she said, It's beautiful.'

The old man shrugged, 'It was never a big success as a slave plantation, it was too small. When I bought it, it had been empty and neglected for years, I like to think I rescued it and stopped it being demolished.'

He rose to his feet, 'Come over here,' he ordered.

Emma followed him as he walked forward about twenty-five yards, and stopped. They were on the edge of an escarpment, and below them, half a mile away was the sea. It was shining blue and gold, from the sun, and you could see the coast extending to left and right of the view.

'It's simply breath-taking, you must love it here,' was all Emma could say. The view alone made this place worth an absolute fortune, her conveyancing head said.

'I love it alright, it's cost me a fortune to get it renovated and how I wanted, but it's been worth every cent. My only regret is my wife didn't live to see it.'

'I'm sorry, said Emma, 'you lost her before it was ready?'

'It's a long time ago now,' was all he said, and turning, walked back to the shade.

CHAPTER TWELVE

The email from her brother Alan was waiting for her when she got in from her swim.

'Hi sis, he wrote. 'How would you feel if I came out for a holiday? The boss says all holidays have to be taken before the end of March, and the weather here is so miserable the only thing I could think of is coming out to see you for ten days or so. Let me know if it's convenient.'

Emma suddenly felt quite homesick, not for the home she had left, but it would be lovely to see her brother again. He had taught her to drive in his spare time, using the old cars he was repairing, and had paid for her driving test. In his own way, he had tried to help. He and Robert had made their escape, but Emma had been left behind with the mother who begrudged every penny spent, and thought any leisure activity which involved spending money was extravagant.

She had Mrs Bristow's lovely little house and a beautiful island to show him, a comfortable spare room he could use, and he could help her buy a little car, an idea which had been at the back of her mind for some time.

She sat down to reply immediately, of course he could come. 'First thing is a passport,' she wrote, You'll need to apply immediately.'

'Already got one!' came the swift reply. 'Been to Sweden with the Boss to the Volvo Plant, and to the Motor Show in Munich.'

'Well, don't pack winter clothes or sweaters, you need shorts, tshirts, trunks and make sure they're made of cotton!' was all she said.

I'm not the only one, who has come a long way, she thought with a smile.

Two weeks later she was standing in arrivals at Grantley Adams waiting for the Gatwick flight to disgorge its passengers. The walk from the plane, the long queue at Immigration, the arrival of luggage which could be slow and the usual crush to get through Customs meant there was a large crowd standing outside in the warm dark waiting for passengers. Most travellers coming through were heading straight for the travel couriers, holding up their company name boards to attract attention. She soon spotted Alan, looking a little lost as he left the air-conditioning behind, and the tropical heat hit.

'Hello bruv.' She said, giving him a peck.

He stared at her in amazement, 'Sis, you look bloody amazing, you've lost weight and you're, well, elegant!'

'Salads, fruit, exercise and most of all, I'm so happy.' she told him, as they walked across the car park and collected her hire car. Toby had offered her his, but as Alan was here for ten days she felt she really couldn't deprive him of his transport as well as taking time off, and having done a good deal with one of the Bridgetown car hire firms she had hired it initially for one week and put both herself and Alan on the insurance.

She drove him home through the warm dark, made a light meal and Alan was soon fighting sleep.

'Go to bed, she said, 'you'll be awake at the crack of dawn for a few days, jet lag.'

Next morning she took him on her usual walk to the beach, he marvelling at the warmth and sunshine, 'So different from January in the UK,' he said. Her regular beach attendant quickly brought another lounger when he saw she had company and grinned as he said. 'You got a man, Miss Emma?'

She laughed, 'Joe, it's my brother, when I get a man, I shan't bring him here, you'll scare him away!'

The boy laughed, he liked this English lady, who always tipped and said thank-you, and in return he kept an eye out for her.

They swam together, something they had not done since they were small children, and then in a cold British sea.

Alan could not get over the warmth, 'it's like a warm bath!' he gasped.

Emma laughed, 'Wait until it rains, you just go for a swim until it stops, the locals call it liquid sunshine.'

For two days she drove them around the island, driving up the wild east coast, where the Atlantic rollers crashed on the shores. Few people lived on this coast, but it was a spectacular sight. They visited old rum plantations, an orchid garden and caves where once long ago escaping slaves would hide in the darkness. These days a little train took visitors through a warren of stalagmites and stalactites, but it was still possible to understand how very dark and frightening they must have been.

They dined at the Club as they were so far north, and Emma was able to introduce Alan to several of her new friends, including Sandy who was going through some designs with the man who had laughed the night she had danced with Charles Brown. As they were also booked in for dinner, they made a table of four and then never stopped talking. Alan entertained them with tales of the old bangers he had restored and some of their hilarious breakdowns.

Bill Pearce the builder, she had finally discovered his name, told them of his early clients when he had first arrived on the island and had to take absolutely any job going in order to survive. Sandy capped it all by describing the client who chased her all over the house before she escaped out of a bathroom window.

Emma could have told the story of walking the length of two bus stops every day to save 10p. But remained silent, even now months later, it was still no laughing matter. So she told the story of meeting Toby and the long length of string which lifted the ground floor door latch when Toby pulled the cord at the side of his desk one floor above.

It was a great night, and her brother remarked as they drove home, that he could perfectly understand how she had fallen in love with the life, it was so very different to the cold unloving poverty she had endured for years and years.

Alan dropped her off at the office next morning. Moving clients around to give herself two free days had meant a busy day in front of her and he promised to be there to pick her up at the end of the day. His job was to go around the garages and try to find her a small, air-conditioned automatic car, preferably low mileage and almost new, she told him. 'Would you like to specify colour as well?' he asked with a grin as he drove away.

Her first job was to read the yellow post-it notes stuck all over her desk, including one from Charles Brown asking her to call in and see him. Emma pulled a face, it could be bad news or good. Alan's arrival had almost made her forget she had an immigration problem. Switching on the coffee machine she pulled her computer towards her and began to wade through the accumulated pile of documents.

By the end of the afternoon she had made a noticeable dent in the heap of documents and switching off the computer went down to find Alan patiently waiting for her with the car's air conditioning keeping everything cool.

'We have to call at a client's house on the way home,' she told Alan, and explained the problem they had with immigration and her taking a job. 'I'm hoping CB has sorted it, I simply never gave it a thought, and now we've had to apply retrospectively.'

Alan grinned. 'It's the sheltered life we've both lived.' He told her 'no holidays, no trips, no foreign parts, we simply didn't realise how things work, the trouble with you and me Sis. is we've no street cred!'

CB was sat in his usual shady spot, and once he realised Emma had company, insisted Alan come in and join them. Emma made the introductions and then went off to find Daisy, his housekeeper and collect another glass for Alan. She stayed chatting for a few minutes, then picking up the glass and a new jug of squash she returned and was surprised to find neither of them there.

Following the sound of voices she went around the house and stopped in amazement. The big double garage doors were open and inside was the largest car she had ever seen. Obviously American, and obviously very old, even Emma could see it was in beautiful condition and had been lovingly cared for. It sat in its spotless garage, its white wall tyres lifted just above ground level, and its paintwork, a beautiful shade of deep blue, gleamed. It looked as though it should belong to an Indian Maharaja or even royalty. There was no sign of her brother, other than a pair of legs sticking out from underneath the car.

'He's admiring the car.' Said CB.

'What? From underneath?' said Emma totally perplexed.

'I think he's looking for a number, he seems to know what he's doing.'

'So he should,' said Emma, 'he got the oldest banger you have ever seen, and by doing it up, and getting it roadworthy, he sold it and repeated the process, again and again. He now has a beautiful modern car in England, but his real love is still old cars.'

Alan emerged grinning, his once white shirt covered in dust and oil stains. 'It's a Cadillac convertible and it's simply beautiful and so well maintained. With your permission Sir, can I do some research on it? I can get on the internet and find out just how rare it is, if I could call in daylight I could find the chassis number and have a really good look at the engine.'

Charles Brown was delighted, not only did no-one ever address him as 'Sir', he had found someone interested in his old car. 'Call me CB, he said 'that's what Emma has christened me, and of course you can come back. I was thinking of letting it go for scrap, but it's in such good condition I couldn't let it go.'

Alan looked horrified, 'Scrap! I don't want to raise your hopes, but I think you may find this is much more valuable than you realise. Sixty year old cars, in this condition...... well, I need to do some research.' was all he could say.

The men were so excited with their discovery Emma had to remind them twice that they had been requested to call, and was it about her Visa?

'Oh that, said CP airily, 'It's in the file by my chair, all signed. I explained to Frank you were not working for any payment, and you were also involved in training on new methods and systems.

Now you have an eleven-month visa you can get Toby to start paying you. Perhaps it got to the top of the pile a bit quicker than normal, but it's all above board and legal.'

They sat in the warm darkness, Alan and CB talking cars, Emma just enjoying the relief and the knowledge that for almost the next year she could remain here and watch Toby's practice grow.

It wasn't until they were actually on their way home that Alan remembered to tell her he had found her a car which he thought would be perfect.

'We'll go see it in the morning,' said Emma.

'Errr, can we leave it until the day after, I promised CB I'll be back first thing, with my research results.

Which is how she came to be back in the office next day, and her brother, having been up half the night on the internet, got her to drop him off at CB's, before she went to work. He was out of the car and half way up the drive, with his laptop under his arm, before she had time to say goodbye.

CHAPTER THIRTEEN

Toby couldn't stop laughing, deserted by her brother who preferred an old car. He had heard about the huge car, over the years, he told Emma, but it came out so rarely it had almost become a legend. The problem Charles had was there was only one dual carriageway in Barbados and most of the roads were simply too small for an enormous car.

Later she was to discover he had acquired it in payment for rent arrears. The 'Jack-the-Lad' who had imported it from the States had regarded it as a status symbol, until he discovered it didn't really suit Bajan roads and cost a fortune to run, then he had been glad to dispose of it in lieu of rent.

Charles' pride meant he couldn't possible admit he had acquired a white elephant, so it had continued to be wheeled out for carnivals and festivals, weddings and important occasions. In between times it was housed in its own garage and regularly cleaned, oiled, maintained and generally cosseted.

Emma drove back at the end of the day, expecting to pick up Alan, only to discover Daisy had set the lovely old dining room for three and they were invited to stay for dinner. It appeared Alan had spent half the day on the phone and the other half under the bonnet of the Cadillac.

CB mixed gin and tonics and they watched the sun set as Alan brought them up to date with his findings. He waited until they were sitting down with their drinks and looking at him expectantly.

'It's a 1959 Cadillac Eldorado Biarritz Convertible, incredibly low mileage, full service history and it's worth a great deal of money. I've spoken to my boss in England, and he passed me on to an expert he knows, they suggested contacting one of the big American auction houses. Most of the big cars finished up in Cuba or somewhere in South America, they used them as taxis, but to find one in this condition is very rare. If it is as good as I think, it will probably go to a Motor Museum.'

There was a stunned silence, no-one had even dreamed of this outcome.

'I hate to sound negative, but all this is assuming CB wants to sell it, he's had it an awful long time.' said Emma.

'Years and years, I've still got the paperwork! Which goes to show you should never throw anything away.' He leaned forward, putting a look of avarice on his face, and rubbing his hands together, 'How much?'

'You look like Uriah Heap,' said Emma laughing.

'Approximately a quarter of a million dollars, depending on the Auction's opinion of its condition,' Alan replied.

That wiped the smiles off everyones faces.

'Say it again,' said Emma quietly.

'About a quarter of a million dollars, give or take,' he repeated.

CB just sat and stared at them both. 'And I almost let it go for scrap value,' was all he said.

This changed everything, Alan rang the UK next morning and got permission from his boss to take another two weeks off, this would be unpaid leave. Emma rang Virgin and exchanged his ticket for the later date. She understood her brother, he simply could not bear to leave without being involved in his discovery and what they would do next.

The main issue, Emma kept reminding them, was what did Charles Brown want to do.

Next morning they called at the local car dealers and Emma took the car Alan had found for her for a spin. It was a perfectly ordinary smart little BMW, it would be sturdy enough for the crowded rush hour roads and had air conditioning and an automatic gear box. Just what she wanted. As it would be a cash purchase, Alan negotiated what he knew to be the best possible price for the vehicle, and the paperwork was soon completed. They arranged for it to be valeted, filled with fuel and delivered to Mrs Bristow's home, the next day.

They then drove up to CB's. Last night Emma had suggested he sleep on the matter and decide what he wanted to do. 'It's your property,' she had told him. 'I'm not going to allow Alan, his boss, or an American Auction house to pressure you. We do nothing until you decide. You've had it an awful long time, perhaps there are sentimental reasons for keeping it.'

They had almost convinced themselves he would say no, it wasn't for sale at any price.

In fact, to their astonishment, it was quite the opposite, he had a long list of questions on how it would be done and where it would go, but he was unshakeable, he wanted rid of it.

Toby was quite right, thought Emma, he's kept it because he was embarrassed, it was a bad deal, and now he has a wonderful reason to part with it.

Alan was to ring the Auction House that had been recommended, it was in Scottsdale, Arizona, he would explain what they had, its age and condition and subject to price, that they were prepared to sell. The photos he had taken would be sent on-line to give them some idea.

On Toby's advice, they were to keep it quiet. Extra garage locks and a small camera would be installed, Alan's technical skills coming in useful as usual.

They did not have to wait long, a phone call to Alan's mobile next morning from Scottsdale explained they had a member of their staff on his way from Cuba to the USA, he had been instructed to change his flight plans and he would be with them tomorrow. Would there be anyone to meet him?

Alan stood in Arrivals at Grantley Adams Airport just as Emma had done almost two weeks earlier, he was holding up a card with MATTHEW ADAMS written in bold letters. He imagined he was looking for a young, fast talking, sharp suited salesman who would be hoping for another chunk of commission. The man who came to greet him was small, grey haired, middle aged, wearing jeans and a battered leather jacket and carrying nothing but a hold-all.

'Not what you expected,' he said with a grin when they had shaken hands.

Alan looked embarrassed, 'Thought they'd send a Salesman,' he muttered.

The man laughed, 'Call me Matt,' he said. 'No point in a fancy salesman, he'd get his nice suit dirty when it came to going under the car. I'm quite capable of negotiating, but my job is to go through your car with a fine tooth comb and tell you what it's worth.'

By the time Alan had dropped him off at the Hilton and arranged to pick him up next morning they were talking shop like old friends. Both had learnt to make-do and mend cars from scratch, there was thirty years difference in their ages but they both had exactly the same skills.

Next morning Matt stood outside the big garage as Alan pushed the doors apart. Spotlessly clean, polished and with its metalwork gleaming thanks to Alan's administrations, the car appeared to almost float above them. Regal and grand, it was like an elderly Duchess waiting for her staff to compliment her.

Matt said absolutely nothing, his training was to show no eagerness or enthusiasm before an inspection, but inside himself, he already knew, here was something very special.

CB had shaken his hand, waved them both in the direction of the garage, and gone off to organise coffee. It was, Alan thought, as though he was waiting to be disappointed.

The two men broke for coffee, then had to be almost prised off the vehicle for the lunch Daisy had provided. At 4.00pm they re-joined CB, who opened two small beers for them and said, 'right, tell me the worst, it's not worth much after all, is it?'

Matt laughed, 'It's years since I saw anything in such great condition, you really have looked after it, Sir,' he told CB. 'Alan is quite right, you have a gem of a vehicle, and it's worth whatever the market will pay, but we're looking at a quarter of a million dollars, even more if there is a fight for it, it really is museum quality.'

The silence whist they absorbed this information was broken by the arrival of Emma, who admitted she simply had to come and see what they had found and had left work early to call and be nosey.

57

CB laughed at her, but then sat and observed her organisational skills as she called a meeting for next day which would include Toby. 'You don't just let it disappear overseas without legal assurances and a decent contract. We need shipping details, auction dates, journey times, commission rates and transport costs. What happens if it doesn't reach our reserve, how will it get to Arizona? Who pays the insurance? Her questions went on and on, and the old man realised she was right they needed a lawyer to talk them through the Contract.

That night Alan, Matt and herself dined at the Club, having arranged to meet Toby there, once he had locked up the Office. Poor Matt spent so much time answering questions he could barely eat his meal, but this would save time tomorrow when they completed the legal formalities.

They held their meeting at Charles Brown's home. Matt was waiting for his offices to open, the three hour time difference in Arizona meant he would be able to tell them he had done the deal and they could begin the process of getting the car to Scottsville. It would be containered, he said, it was far too valuable to go any other way. It would travel on a Container ship, through the Panama and then remain in its box until it arrived at the Auction House. Here it would be thoroughly gone over, cleaned and polished and put on display as the prize item in one of their huge exhibition halls which attracted buyers from all over the world.

Toby had proved his worth, going through every word of the Contract and ensuring they had everything covered. He conceded in the end, the Auction House had done this thousands of times, it was a fair proposal from a world-famous company who had a great reputation and he recommended Charles to sign on the dotted line.

She saw very little of her brother after that, despite his extended stay. He and Matt had paid a visit to the main Harbour outside Bridgetown and made all the arrangements at this end. The ship which was to carry the car would have come across the Atlantic from Europe, dropping off its cargo in several other Caribbean islands, call in at Columbia and would then continue through the Panama and travel up the west coast of the USA.

When they weren't busy with shipping documents, they prepared the car for its journey.

'Treating it as if they were swaddling a new born,' Emma had said.

Coming in late one evening, Alan dropped his bombshell, Matt was to fly back to Arizona once the car was safely loaded, 'What would you think, if I said I was going with him?' he had asked her.

Emma looked at him, he was twenty-eight, single, solvent and had seen little or nothing of pleasure during his childhood. 'I would say go,' she said. 'If you don't do it now, you will probably regret it forever, old cars and you are made for each other!'

The relief on his face told her all she needed to know, and he went on to explain the plan.

Matt had done five years of travelling, inspecting, and rejecting in many cases, old cars from all over the Americas. He had met a lady he wanted to settle down with and had told his employers it was time he retired and took a job in the office. He was tired of the endless travelling, it was a task which required a younger man, who really needed to be single and without a family. Finding the single person was easy, finding someone who had the knowledge to assess and value old vehicles was much harder. He had spoken to his office, telling them he thought he may have found just the person, and now he wanted Alan to fly back and spend a week in the Auction House with him. If he didn't like what he saw, he flew home. If he thought he could do the job, with Matt training him over the next few months, he would have a contract and a salary larger than he had ever imagined.

'You have Barbados, that is your magic,' he told Emma,' but this is mine, I can't say no.'

CHAPTER FOURTEEN

The procession approaching Bridgetown on its way to the Harbour had everyone staring. Here was the biggest car most of them had ever seen, making its way through the town with Charles Brown sitting proudly in the passenger seat, whilst Matt drove the vehicle carefully through the crowded roads. Alan and Emma followed behind in her BMW, it felt like a royal progress, and when CB began to wave to the pedestrians who had stopped to stare, she didn't know if she wanted to laugh or join in and wave also.

The car had to be loaded in the dockyard, the container simply would not have gone through the stone gates of his home and this was the answer. Matt had eased it gently into the large container which was waiting with its doors wide open, then supervised, as it was secured and tightly strapped down in case of bad weather. Layers of rubber were wrapped around it, until Emma thought it was beginning to look like an Egyptian mummy, and then the huge steel box was carefully locked and sealed. It would not be opened again until it reached its destination.

They watched as the giant crane swung it gently into the air to join a stack of other waiting containers. It would be a seventeen-day journey through the Panama Canal until it reached San Diego, where it would then be transported by road to its destination.

'Well, that's the end of that, I shan't see it again.' its owner said, as he watched the crane gently set it down.

It was Matt who turned to him and said, 'Why ever not? Most owners come along and watch the fun, particularly when it's a special sale. An auction can be really exciting. Once you know the date of your auction you can fly to Florida, change planes to Arizona, and we can pick you up from the airport. We do it all the time.'

There was a stunned silence and the old man simply turned and walked back to where Emma was waiting.

Alan and Matt had squeezed into the back of her small car, CB having pride of place in the front passenger seat. Once they got to the airport, they got him out first and then Alan and Matt literally crawled out, dragging Matt's holdall after them, Alan's big case having taken up most of the space in the boot. Shaking hands with CB, and giving his sister a peck on the cheek the two men were off. Now the car was safely on its way, Matt couldn't wait to get back to his home town and show Alan the ropes.

CB watched them go. 'Huh, fancy suggesting I should go to the Auction, never heard anything like it' was his first comment as she drove out of the airport.

Emma hid a smile, if he hadn't wanted to go, he would never have mentioned it again, but here he was making it the first topic of conversation.

'Well, Matt wouldn't have mentioned it if it wasn't a regular occurrence, people obviously do like to go and see how much their car makes, or who buys it. It might be someone quite famous, or even a well-known museum.'

'Well, I can't go, and that's that.'

'Let me guess,' said Emma, 'you don't have a passport, you couldn't get a US Visa, you can't afford the air fare or you're just plain scared?'

There was long pause. 'Just plain scared, I've never flown, never been off the island, now I come to think about it.' This was said in a very small voice.

Perhaps it was time for some honesty, Emma thought. 'I had never flown when I came to Barbados, but I enjoyed all seven and a half hours of the flight. If I can manage that, surely you can manage two much shorter flights, it's only four hours to Florida and Jet Blue means you change flights there.'

There was a second long pause. 'Anyway, I haven't got a passport.'

'Your friend Frank, will soon solve that problem.' Emma said.

This time the pause was even longer. 'How do you get a US Visa?'

'The travel-agent does that for you.' She said.

Another long pause. 'I couldn't possible go alone, I'm too old to travel.'

'You could take a companion.' She was thinking of Daisy, though what the Housekeeper's husband, who did all the gardening and handyman jobs would say, she wasn't sure.

This time there was no pause at all....

'Well, that's settled then, you'll have to book both our flights and get some hotel rooms, and we need the best seats on the plane, I'll leave it to you.'

Emma was thunderstruck, this hadn't been what she had meant at all.

'Me? I didn't mean me. I can't go, I'm working for Toby.' This was the only excuse she could think of at that moment.

'If he wants my business, he'll not mind. Besides I'm thinking of you, you'll want to see your brother.'

'I've just seen my brother! CB, I can't go flying off to America with you, they might think I was your daughter, or even worse your fancy woman! I wasn't inviting myself along, honestly.'

He shrugged his shoulders. 'Well, I'm not going unless you go with me, so it will be your fault if I miss the sale of my lovely old car, and that will probably break my heart.'

'Is this the lovely old car you were thinking of selling for scrap? How times have changed! It's blackmail.' she said, beginning to feel quite angry. She was being manipulated.

In the end she dropped him off at his home and agreed reluctantly to think about it. Secretly she was hoping Toby would step in and say no, he couldn't possibly do without her.

Some hope. When he had stopped laughing Toby said. 'But, of course, you have to go. There's more to this than you think,' Emma, he told her. ' He has no family, worked hard all his life, had little time for fun and just as he was making a real success and some real money his wife died and left him alone. Daisy and her husband got him organised and have looked after him for years, but he never wanted to remarry, he's remained alone. You and Alan, and Matt, even myself in a funny way, we've all given him a new interest in life. Think about it Emma, he knows your skills and has confidence in you getting him there and back, he simply won't go without you.'

Very reluctantly, Emma agreed she would indeed, think about it.

CHAPTER FIFTEEN

And then two weeks later came the phone call. Could Emma possibly call on her way home? Before dark if possible, there was something he would like to show her. She had not seen CB since the day Alan and Matt had left and was hoping he might have forgotten their conversation, he certainly didn't mention it as she picked him up and he directed her towards one of the larger villages just outside Bridgetown.

Here at the junction of two roads was a small community of shops, placed just far enough from the road for two lines of car parking in front. To one side were the remnants of fruit and vegetable stalls, which were empty today. There was a supermarket, a jewellery store, two shops selling wraps and dresses and at one end a double fronted empty shop with a large gate leading to a yard at one side.

Emma looked at him perplexed. 'What am I supposed to think, why are you showing me this, is it yours?'

He ignored the question and answered impatiently, 'Well of course it is, I'm showing you because it's ideal for your business. You and Toby Ogle get a room each, and it's big enough for you to take on another employee when you expand, or you could have a receptionist.' Then it dawned on her, this man was offering her some out of town premises, did they want to be out of town? Was it to buy, they couldn't afford it. Was it to rent? If so, how much? And what on earth would Toby say?

Upstairs was obviously occupied, the windows washed and newly painted.

CB shifted, slightly embarrassed to show a softer side. ' I've hung on to it because there's a good tenant upstairs and I don't want to lose him. He's converted upstairs into a lovely flat for himself, and uses the yard for his work, he's away during the day, and his dog secures the place at night.'

Emma agreed, but pointed out that Toby was trying hard to build a new practice and it was the only place in Bridgetown they could afford.

'Nonsense, you don't need to be in Bridgetown, you just need a bus route or ample parking, you can't park down there for love or money. How many of your clients come by car?'

'Well, most of them,' admitted Emma.

The old man smiled. 'Offices, there's a small washroom and kitchenette at the back and you could divide the front into two nice offices and an entrance hall. It would need a bit of work, but its the right size and there's even a small reception where you could keep your clients waiting! Parking at the side for you both and someone living upstairs to keep an eye on it at night.'

'Offices,' she thought. Exactly what they needed, the current premises were on their last legs, water came in when it rained heavily, the clients complained about the steep stairs and Toby and herself were falling over files and records which had simply nowhere to go.

'Come on, before it's too dark to see properly.' He picked up his bunch of keys and got out of the car. The door obviously hadn't been opened for a long time, it smelt musty and warm, there was no air conditioning here. Apart from a pile of old junk mail it was clean and tidy, the old shop counter still dominating the room, probably too big to remove, she thought. He was right, it would need work to divide up the interior, but it was quite big enough and there was also a small extension to the rear built under a metal fire escape which led upstairs, this would be perfect for secure storage.

They were still inspecting the place when there was the sound of an engine and she looked up to see a lorry drawing up to the gates. A man got out to open them accompanied by a large dog, they jumped back in the lorry and drove slowly into the yard at the rear. Closing the gates and leaving his dog behind he came straight into the shop. It was Bill Pearce, the man who she had met several times at the club, but had not known he was a tenant of CB's. Once he saw it was Charles Brown he relaxed.

'Sorry, just wanted to check who was in the place. Oh, it's you Emma, didn't recognise the car, how are you?'

64

'I'm fine, she told him, 'CB is just showing me around, we were thinking offices.'

Bill nodded thoughtfully, 'It would make sense, the proportions would work and I'd certainly like to quote for it.'

'Before we do anything, we have to convince Toby, he will say we can't afford it. It won't just be structural, there's new furniture and desks, publicity, advertising, decorating, signage, removal costs, in fact everything but the kitchen sink to factor in.'

Bill grinned, 'You'll need a kitchen sink as well, it's pretty awful.'

'We can perhaps come to some arrangement, but Emma's right, we need to let Toby have a look at it.' CB said.

Emma realised why he had approached her first, she was obviously the one who had to convince Toby.

'Emma, we can't afford it.' She knew exactly what he would say and he did.

'Look, Emma said, 'just come and look, we can then walk away, but we need to know what he has in mind. At the moment he is getting no income at all from the empty premises, but if he got a decent tenant, even at a cheap rent, it would be better than nothing at all.'

Very reluctantly Toby agreed to just go and look. With the borrowed keys she walked him through the old shop giving him a commentary on her ideas for breaking up the area and how it would work. A central door leading to a small reception, and space behind for two decent size offices, A new kitchenette and washroom at the rear, and most important storage!

Parking to the side, it was on the bus route, and security by night because Bill lived upstairs, and it would be quiet during the day when he was away working. Bill Pearce had converted upstairs into a lovely flat for himself, and that meant he could keep an eye on his yard, which had experienced several thefts from his previous premises. Now he and his dog lived over the shop, he no longer had that worry. Plus the traffic of Bridgetown would not be tearing past their windows as it currently did.

'Emma, I already owe you a fortune, how are we going to pay for this?'

'We're going up to CB's for a drink, and we tell him the truth, we're hard up, but it's marvellous and just what we need.' she said.

Charles Brown sat and listened to their story, he was well aware they were a new practice and still working to grow their clients. He had known all along exactly what he would do, but had no intentions of letting them think it was a long standing plan, he would play this his way.

'I'm tired of seeing it vacant, it doesn't do the neighbourhood any good to see empty premises' he said. 'Suppose we help each other out, get Bill to quote for the structural work, stud walls, doors, new kitchen and washroom, electrics etc. I'll settle his bills. You pay for the glamorous bits, furniture, paint, paper, advertising etc. Get that girl friend of yours to design it, Toby.'

This was way more than they had ever hoped for. If the structural work was paid by their future landlord, they were sure they could manage the rest. They could even do some of the painting and decorating themselves. Giddy with excitement they planned a time-line, first job being quotes from Bill. Secondly, they needed to involve Sandy, she had a gift for making things look wonderful on a shoestring.

As they said their goodbyes, intent on driving straight up to the Club to find her and Bill, CB leant forward through the car window.

'How are you getting on with planning our trip, Emma? Have you heard from Alan on an auction date yet?'

Meeting Toby's eyes for a moment, she said, 'I'll give him a ring tomorrow CB, and let you know.'

'Well, said Toby as they pulled away, 'if ever there was a trade-off, this is it!'

CHAPTER SIXTEEN

Sandy's visit next evening began badly when she checked off all the mundane things they hadn't given any thought to. An air conditioning system, it would need a burglar alarm and a new boiler.

Sandy measured the rooms, this would give them an idea of desk sizes, and they could get a settee and coffee table in one corner.

Toby rolled his eyes. 'New desks? Security system? Settee? Hang on Sandy, we've no money for that sort of makeover.'

'Yes, we have.' said Emma. If I'm going to get my Long-Term Work Permit, it means I'm going to be here for quite a while, and we might as well work in comfort. I'll settle your bill for the makeover Sandy, Toby can pay me back monthly as the Practice grows, we can do it legally with a written agreement.'

Toby's jaw dropped, 'Emma, it's a very generous offer, but I can't accept it.'

Sandy broke into the argument, 'Toby, silly as it might sound, a bright modern office which gives an impression of a successful business, is just what you need. The facelift will help the business to grow.'

As they had a final look around Sandy said, 'We can't leave without seeing Bill, he will want to be involved.'

There was a small door set inside the large gates, for some reason Emma thought it was called a Judas door and there was a doorbell attached. Toby rang it and eventually they heard footsteps coming down the outside staircase at the side of the shop.

'Come on upstairs,' Bill said. 'Excuse the mess, I've just arrived home.'

It wasn't a mess at all, it was a long room, open plan, with the kitchen at one end. It was divided into sections by the use of a table and further down the room two long settees facing each other. Mainly in cream, the room had flashes of navy and maroon in the cushions and rug, with one statement wall containing all the other colours. It was restful and comfy, but still had a masculine edge to it. Emma loved it.

They settled on the couches whilst Bill opened a bottle of wine. Sandy explained she had known Bill for several years and always tried to use him for her projects, the room they were in was one of her designs. Trouble was, he was now so well known, she had to wait longer and longer until he was free.

Bill was delighted that someone might be interested in taking downstairs, and he thought a solicitors practice would suit both Toby and himself. He would be out all day, once he had loaded up each morning it was rare for him to return before six. At night he put the dog in the yard, where it had a luxurious kennel, built by himself, and they had security for both residences. His thefts had ceased the moment he moved and he was happy here.

Bill and Toby were soon deep in plans and conversation, Bill was sketching out his ideas on a pad he had borrowed from Sandy. The two girls were obviously excluded from all this 'men's talk' and Emma found herself confiding in Sandy about her forthcoming trip to Scottsdale.

'I really have been bulldozed into this and just don't know where to start, it's Arizona, he'll need hotels, airport transfers, it will be hot even in the spring, he has never left the island before, never gone through immigration, he wants the best seat on the plane and insists I'm going with him!'

Sandy looked thoughtful, 'I don't know much about it, but I know there's a new scheme with VIP transfers and escorted travel. Why don't you talk to Melanie, she runs the travel agency I always use for my trips and she's great with making things as easy as possible for her older customers. So many of them make the trip to England to visit their children and grandchildren, so she's used to finding flights which go at reasonable times and with easy transfers.'

By the time they had consumed the second bottle of wine a deal had been struck. Sandy would design and oversee the makeover of the property, Bill would carry out any structural changes she required and Emma would pay the bill for the moment. Only Toby was unhappy.

'I can't let you do it Emma,' he said, as he drove her home. 'What if it fails, you will have lost your investment.'

'Then you will have lost your livelihood, we're not going to fail, what we're going to do is introduce some of the more modern ideas and practices the UK are using. We're going to have a grand opening, full newspaper coverage, start advertising on local radio and put ourselves forward as a young, progressive and thoroughly switched on practice!' Here she paused, she had run out of breath.

She drove over to see Charles Brown with her news, 'Yes, please, we would love to be your tenants.' He sat back and beamed. 'Bill Pearce is going to do the alterations and Sandy will design the interior,' she told him. 'We want to show ourselves as a young progressive practice, crikey, she thought, I'm beginning to believe it myself.'

The old man looked thoughtful, 'If I waive the first quarter's rent, will that help pay for the alterations and fittings?'

Emma leaned forward and impulsively kissed him on the cheek. 'You're a love, she said, 'That will help a lot.'

'Mind you, I want to be invited to the opening party.' He said, gruffly.

'You're not only invited, you're the guest of honour, you get to cut the ribbon!'

Bit by bit the plan had come together. Sandy produced sketches and colour swatches, and these were accepted immediately. Emma liked her grey and silver scheme, it was business like and striking, with red flashes at the same time livening the overall effect. Caterers were chosen, they would use the Club staff and the opening date was finally agreed, she thought Sandy had grasped instantly the image they wanted. She called one lunchtime to find men in face masks with a huge machine sanding floors, it was impossible to see for the dust and after taking one look she drove back to work.

Although Sandy had gone for a modern look in her design, she took Toby and Emma to a second hand furniture sale. It was a huge building, full of tables, chairs, cupboards, benches, everything you could possibly need to furnish a house or office. 'Brown furniture is out of fashion,' she told them. 'It's going cheap, but big pieces are cheaper still. If we can find the right shapes and size we can paint or stain them, add new leather tops and handles and get the look without the cost.'

As they had different offices, the desks didn't need to be identical and she found them two large plain desks, she could renovate. Two small very scruffy settees, totally different colours, but identical in size and shape came next. Then a marble topped table with broken legs, 'new short legs, that's your coffee table.' They came away, having spent a lot less than expected and feeling slightly shell shocked. It was up to Sandy now to collect the items, and have them painted, stained, re-upholstered and whatever else was required.

The newly sanded floor was stained a lovely shade of red mahogany and the walls papered in a soft grey sea-grass paper. When the newly renovated desks arrived Emma barely recognised them, black and shining with new paint and inset blotters of scarlet leather. The two settees had been covered in a soft grey velour, they made a right-angle around the coffee table on its new short black metal legs. Chairs had been covered in the bright red of the leather desk tops and could be moved from room to room as required.

The plain wall in the entrance had been set aside for their qualifications and Sandy had had them reframed in scarlet, and hung where waiting clients could study them. Emma's certificates had been one of the items she had almost thrown away, now retrieved from her brother's home in London they were to be hung here on the wall.

She arrived one day to find the night security shutters had been fitted, this was an expense Toby hadn't wanted, but as Sandy pointed out, two huge plate glass windows would be very expensive to replace if some late night reveller decided to demolish them.

The plate glass windows had been cleaned until they shone. Winnie and a friend had been in and cleaned the place from top to bottom. The new chairs were due any day.

The sign writer had arrived with his gold paint and proceeded to fill the glass with his writing. TOBY OGLE, SOLICITORS it said across both windows, he then painted a list running down the side of each window setting out the number of different tasks the practice undertook.

Capital Gains Tax, Inheritance Tax Planning, Wills, Contracts, Lifetime Trusts, Probate, Divorce, Separation, Child custody – the list seemed endless.

Across the bottom of the windows ran the words Emma Hird, Conveyancing Department.

As well as advertising their skills, this broke up the view into each office and gave them some privacy. When Sandy arrived with a wagon full of plants and potted orchids all in grey, red and black tubs and containers, she filled the floor in front of the windows, and their privacy was ensured.

The decorators had finished to Sandy's satisfaction, the wiring, phones and computers were in, and working. Bill had replaced the old sink with a new kitchenette, comprising a microwave, small sink, room for the coffee machine and an under-counter fridge. One wall had been covered with pegboard, filled with hooks and ready for mugs and cups. It was tiny, but perfectly serviceable and everything was new. The door opposite had previously led to a very old and extremely unhygienic w.c, now there was a new white toilet and a small matching hand basin. The walls were mirror tiles giving the small room the impression of being much larger.

Sandy had got the press on her side and they would be there to help with publicity. The theme of using old retail property and converting it into something smart and useful would be used in the newspaper article. The reporter would have loved to tell the story of the old car and its journey to the States, but CB was adamant it was not to be mentioned, he didn't want the whole of Barbados knowing his business. He did however, agree reluctantly to cut the ribbon at the grand reopening of the old shop.

CHAPTER SEVENTEEN

'What we need now,' said Emma, 'is another pair of hands at this end of the move. You'll be busy at the new place, but I shall be here supervising everything going across on Bill's wagon. Clients files need moving carefully, you can't afford to have them blowing away all over the road. I think I'll ask Joe if he might be interested in some extra work.'

'Joe? Is this a secret boyfriend?' asked Toby with a grin.

Joe is my friend from the beach, he's incredible neat. The lounger beds have to be in straight formal rows or he's not happy. Moving the files might just suit him.'

That teatime she drove up the coast to her usual beach and found Joe stacking beds for the night, as usual they were stacked in a perfectly straight tidy line.

'Bit late for a swim Miss Emma,' he said when he saw her.

Emma explained she wasn't looking for a late swim, but for him.

'Do you work here all the time, or could you take another job on?' she asked.

Joe sat down on one of his lounger beds and looked at her. 'I do this because I can't find an alternative. Skipped most of school because I hated it, found the learning bit easy, it was dodging the bullies that was the problem.'

'So you can read and write competently?' she asked him.

'Can even spell it!' he replied with his usual grin.

Emma explained she was looking for someone for a few days work moving offices and it would mean him taking responsibility for clients files, moving them to the new premises and setting up a filing system at the new place. 'I've watched you stacking chairs, serving in the bar, you're extremely neat and everything is orderly, I think you could do the job.'

Joe grinned, 'Mam says it's my OCD coming out!'

He was waiting for her outside the Bridgetown office next morning. He wore a spotless white Tee shirt and clean jeans and looked very smart.

'Not sure how long we can keep your Tee shirt looking like that,' Emma told him. 'It's extremely dusty in there and some files have not been moved for years.'

She spent the first hour showing him how the coffee machine worked, how to pack the files in alphabetical order, to mark the boxes with the first and last file numbers, and stack them by the door ready for carrying down the steep difficult stairs.

Joe scratched his head, 'What do I put the files in?' he asked.

'That's the very first job,' said Emma, pointing to a huge pile of cardboard. 'You build the boxes from this pile, they all come flat-packed!'

It got better as the day progressed. Once he had built some boxes, he had somewhere to put the files. His clean Tee shirt was soon filthy, but he stopped work only when the sandwiches arrived from a local café. He listened to Emma dealing with phone calls, and asked intelligent questions about conveyancing and how it worked, who was it protecting and where did her information come from.

At the end of the day Emma thought they had packed up half the files, and was satisfied they might finish tomorrow. She gave a very grubby Joe a lift home.

'Black Tee shirt tomorrow', he said as he thanked her and waved goodbye.

True to his word, he arrived promptly wearing black, and whilst Emma made coffee, he began building a further pile of boxes. They worked until lunchtime, once the sandwiches had arrived Joe sat behind Toby's old desk to eat his. 'This is nice.' was all he said.

They had just completely emptied the old storeroom when Bill arrived, with an empty wagon. He and Joe carried down box and box and loaded them into the back.

'it's going to take two trips.' Bill told her. 'I'll be back in the morning first thing, but I could do with a hand at the other end with this lot.'

'I'll come with you.' Joe said, eager to see the new place.
'Are you sure, said Emma, 'it will make you very late home.'
Joe looked at her and grinned. 'It's overtime Miss Em, it's great.'

Later, Bill told Emma about the rest of his evening. Joe had been fine until he met Killer, and had turned a dreadful shade of grey. He had been bitten as a small boy and been terrified of dogs ever since. To begin with he wouldn't even leave the cab of the lorry.

Bill had taken him up to the flat, made them both a drink and got Killer to sit quietly in the corner. As the dog had just eaten his dinner he was perfectly happy to sit and snooze. Then leaving the files locked in the yard they had taken Killer for a walk, and Joe was able to watch the animal run off some energy and retrieve the ball they threw for him.

By the time they had unloaded the lorry, and locked up again, it was dark, and they were both hungry. They stopped off at a Bajan bar on their way to take Joe home and enjoyed freshly caught Mahi mahi and rice, Killer sitting under the table hoping for titbits.

It would take time, Bill had said, but he was sure they had made a start on conquering Joe's fear of dogs.

By the official opening day, Joe was almost part of the fixtures and fittings. He had hung pictures and certificates, washed windows, made coffee for numerous workmen and delivery folk, and rearranged the files in the new strongroom.

It had been the question of the files, which had made Emma rethink her 'just a few days work'

He had queried why they were all the same colour, why they were not simply on the computer and why they were not categorised.

Emma explained they were obliged to keep hard copies, but the majority of these files were old, some torn and shabby and inherited from the elderly solicitor when he sold the practice to Toby. They probably hadn't been looked at for years and years, but they still had to be retained.

Next time she happened to look in the new strong room she was amazed to find a re-arranged system, all files over a certain age had a bright blue sticker on them and were stacked neatly and alphabetically in a small section away from the current clients. There was also a 'Work in Progress' section, which was red stickered and nearer to the door. They would be moved into general filing and their red spots removed once the files were closed.

'When did you find time to do this?' Emma asked Joe, amazed at the neatness.

Joe grinned, 'Told you before, Ma says it's my OCD!' he said with a laugh.

Slowly, over the next month it all came together. The night security shutters were fitted, this was an expense Toby hadn't wanted, but as Sandy pointed out, two huge plate glass windows would be very expensive to replace if some late night reveller decided to demolish them.

The newly sanded floor was stained a lovely shade of red mahogany and the walls papered in a soft grey sea-grass paper. When the newly renovated desks arrived Emma barely recognised them, black and shining with new paint and inset blotters of scarlet leather. The two settees had been covered in a soft grey velour, they made a right-angle around the coffee table on its new short black metal legs. Chairs had been covered in the bright red of the leather desk tops and could be moved from room to room as required.

The plain wall in the entrance had been set aside for their qualifications and Sandy had had them reframed in scarlet, and hung where waiting clients could study them. Her certificates had been one of the items she had almost thrown away, now retrieved from her brother's home in London they were here on the wall.

The invitations had gone out several days ago, the opening date fixed, the caterers' booked and Toby, Emma, Bill and Sandy sat down together for their final meeting.

Emma reported she was waiting for final acceptance numbers, these she would pass to the Caterers, then she was ready.

Bill said he had one more coat of gloss to put on the smart black and gold exterior, and he was done.

Sandy said the statement paper for one wall of each office, which had been ordered and was coming from the USA had arrived and would be done tomorrow.

Toby said his nervous breakdown was due the same day.

CHAPTER EIGHTEEN

Emma held her breath and hoped everything was covered. Killer had been sent up to CB's where Daisy and her husband would spoil him. The caterers together with Alex, the Club's restaurant manager had set up the drinks and food in the yard, where Bill hoped everyone would admire all Joe's work. There wasn't a tool or piece of building material out of place. In a clever move, Joe had pinned the plans and alterations on a large board, so any potential customers could see just what could be done with old retail property.

On the day of the opening Emma had organised a limo to pick up CB and bring him to the opening party. He had arrived accompanied by two other elderly men, all three of them looking very smart if slightly old-fashioned in their suits. Mr B sat in the front passenger seat, so she took him through the ribbon cutting ceremony once more. 'I know what to do, he said waspishly, 'I've cut ribbons before.'

The yellow ribbon had been placed across the door and a pair of huge dressmakers scissors borrowed. Everyone who had helped had been invited, Winnie and her friend, who had cleaned the place until it shone, arrived in their best clothes and hats. Electricians, sign writers, painters, computer geeks, phone people were all there. Joe's mum had been asked, Emma felt it was important she should realise how much Joe had done, and how he was appreciated. It worked both ways, she had told Emma, in her opinion they had transformed her son from a truculent teenager into a hard working and very happy young man.

Joe himself was everywhere, wearing a new pair of pale grey trousers, an immaculate white shirt and a tie borrowed from Bill, he was meeting, greeting, fetching drinks and ensuring everyone was happy.

CB stood, introduced by Toby as the landlord and owner of the premises. The old man then gave an extremely short speech, for which Emma was thankful. He had teased her the week before by waving several pages of foolscap paper, saying this was his official opening speech!

This time he simply said that an empty property dragged down a neighbourhood and here was an example of what could be done to change that. He encouraged everyone to view not just the new practice, but to see what could be done upstairs thanks to Bill's efforts.

With a flourish of the scissors the ribbon was cut and everyone crowded in to inspect Sandy's stylish designs, which were both modern and businesslike. Sandy herself was delighted to be showing off her work, as it usually led to further commissions.

Toby and Emma were operating the meet and greet, when Sandy said in a hushed voice, 'Do you see whose come?' Emma shook her head, she only knew their immediate clients.

'It's the business men behind the developments in the North of the Island she said, St.Charles, how ever did they get an invite? Her question was answered immediately, CB had brought them. Once they had a drink Charles brought them over to meet Toby and Emma, then on to Bill and Sandy, giving a short resume of each of them, their backgrounds and their skills.

Emma's job was to identify the visitors who were potential customers, future clients would come from the building and leisure industry, larger conveyancing jobs for her, and bigger cases for Toby. She steered several in his direction and he was kept busy answering questions and even managed to make a couple of appointments. The poor visitors would be going home with business cards from Bill, Sandy and Toby's practice, she prayed they would result in more work for all of them.

. The evening was a great success, waiters came forward and encouraged people to the buffet, others chose to walk round the new offices and admire the décor, but by the end of the evening everyone had eaten well and the atmosphere was amazing.

Sandy was seen disappearing upstairs with one visitor, but it turned out she was showing him the apartment she had designed for Bill. Mr.B and his two old cronies had a wonderful time, the old man knew almost everyone there and chatted non stop. Toby and Bill kept an eye on everyone, ensuring their drinks were refilled and they had food.

It wasn't really a night for making appointments or even talking business, it was a night to get to know the people and circulate. Toby and Emma were invited to a drinks party at the Sports Club and accepted immediately. Emma had been right to spend this money Toby thought, it was opening doors.

As they took their leave, one of the St.Charles guests approached Emma, and asked quietly if his secretary could ring her tomorrow for an appointment. 'I have a tricky conveyancing problem, he said. Charles tells me you are London trained and up to date with some of the latest changes and rules, I would like to come and see you.'

'Of course, said Emma, 'I will look forward to hearing from you.'

When Emma saw the club manager talking to Joe, she thought nothing of it, both Bill and herself had sung his praises, and Alex had gone over to introduce himself and chat to the boy.

The first day in the new premises was slightly chaotic. The phones never stopped ringing. People rang to say thank you for the hospitality, or could they make an appointment, flowers and good luck cards kept arriving and Joe was kept busy, needing to dash out several times for yet more milk for the coffee machine. It was late before they finally closed up for the night, and Emma suddenly realised that Joe had been quiet all day and was now hanging about waiting to talk to her.

'Come on, let's give you a lift home, it's been a busy day.' she told Joe. She had long since discovered the best place to hear what was happening was in the car.

Joe settled himself in the passenger seat and said, 'Alex has offered me a job, he needs another waiter and thinks I fit the part.'

Emma looked at him 'Joe that's fabulous, it's a super place to work and I think you'll be great.'

The boy shrugged, 'I can't do it, I don't know a thing about taking orders, serving, mixing drinks, carving meat, I'd get the sack the first day.'

Emma took a deep breath, so much of this boy was herself just over a year ago, untravelled, unsophisticated and naïve.

'Alex is far too good a restaurant manager to let you loose anywhere near the dining room until you've gone through a period of training. You'll probably start in the kitchens, learning how it works, how to plate up, prepare vegetables, clean down at the end of the day. Then you'll have to progress to the next stage, whatever that is. Of course you can do it, you just need training that's all, Alex knows that.'

'Do you think so?' he said doubtfully. 'he said I should go home and think about it and if I had any questions, to come back to him.'

'Right, this is what we do,' said Emma. 'Tomorrow you can use Toby's desk, as he's in court. We send Alex an email with a list of questions. For example, how much training will I get, is there a uniform, does the staff bus run frequently, how much do you pay, and so on. Tonight I suggest you write yourself a list of all the questions and we'll sent it to Alex tomorrow. That way he knows you're keen, you're asking intelligent questions and possibly looking to a future career.'

As she dropped him off outside his home, she leaned forward and said. 'Joe, the most important question of all is, do you want to do it?'

'More than anything, Miss Em. This could be my big chance.' he said quietly.

When Emma arrived at work next morning, Joe was already at Toby's desk typing furiously with two fingers. 'Morning Miss Em, I'm only using Toby's email, nothing else.' He said.

Emma was puzzled, 'How did you know his password' she asked?'

Joe grinned. 'I didn't, but thought about it, and tried SANDY, worked first time!'

Emma returned to her office to hide her smile, this boy would either reach the top or finish up in jail, she thought.

With the help of spellcheck, Joe finished his email to Alex and took it to Emma for approval.

It was well written and more importantly well thought out. The questions were sensible and direct. The final paragraph made it clear to Alex that this was to be a stepping stone to learning a great deal more about the huge tourist industry and how it worked, Joe was ambitious and would work hard to move up the career ladder if they would train him.

CHAPTER NINETEEN

Later that evening she e-mailed Alan, she knew he had flown home via Atlanta with a job offer in his pocket to talk to his Boss. He had been relieved to find his firm already knew. The London expert had heard from Scottsdale and informed Alan's boss that he was likely to lose his best mechanic. Alan was immensely relieved to find he had been quite understanding. The only advice he gave Alan was to hang on to his property, if he got a good tenant it would give him some extra income whilst he was away and he would always have somewhere to come home to.

This was wise advice and Alan soon found a couple of young women from the local Estate Agents who had been looking for somewhere to rent. They had turned down several of the tenancies which came through their office, they were prepared to pay a higher rent to get something which was in a decent area, newly furnished and modern. Alan's place fitted the bill perfectly, and he knew it would be well looked after. He had also found time to take the smaller girl out to dinner. Short, red haired, bubbly and with a wonderful sense of humour, she was just his type, and he rather hoped she might still be here when he finally returned to the UK.

He was to spend a month in the Scottsdale office, then he was going to do two more months on the road with Matt, learning the ropes. Matt would then take up a position based in head office. There was a vacancy coming up for a Display Manager, someone who organised the massive showrooms, got the cars on their stands and looking their best and greeted and advised potential buyers. It would suit Matt right down to the ground.

The Auction was just two weeks away,
'The sooner the better,' Melanie had said when she told her the story. 'Midsummer is seriously hot, into three figures, but it will be quite warm enough in spring. Let me work on this for a couple of days, find some flights, look at hotels and find the

easiest way to do it. If money isn't the issue I think we can do this in comfort, will you leave it with me?'

Emma drove home feeling a bit more reassured about the whole trip. It looked as though she was going whether she wanted to or not.

Later, sitting watching the sunset with a glass of wine, she reflected this was just about the first time for weeks she felt her feet had touched the floor. Alan's visit, the discovery of the car, an eleven-month visa, Matt's arrival, the possibility of new offices, and a trip to Arizona, she felt she hadn't paused since she came back from Miami. And she came here for a holiday!

The moment of relaxation was broken when Winnie came around from next door, 'You're in Emma, never see you these days,' she said. 'Mrs Bristow's rung, her mum has died and she really would like a word with you.'

'Oh God,' thought Emma, 'That's all I need, new accommodation, she'll be coming home!'

It would be bedtime in the UK, so she reluctantly picked up the phone to ring Bournemouth and made suitable noises about the death of Mrs Bristow's mother.

'That's kind of you,' Mrs Bristow said briskly, 'but it's been coming a long time and I've got quite used to the idea that this was the end of her road. I really wanted to talk to you about your tenancy.'

Emma's stomach plummeted, she was going to be turned out.

Mrs Bristow sounded rather hesitant as she continued. 'I've been here so long, I've got friendly with the proprietor of the nursing home, she's ready for retirement, her daughter is going to take over the running of the Home and she's thinking of going on a world cruise. Says it's her first holiday for years, and would I like to go with her. What do you think?'

Emma was totally confused, here she was expecting to be turned out of her lovely Chattel house, and here was Mrs Bristow, asking her advice.

'Do you mean, I can stay here a bit longer?' she asked.

'Yes, if I do a World Cruise, its one hundred and fortyfive days, I won't be home for a while, does that matter?' Mrs Bristow said.

'Not at all, I love it here, and would be delighted to stay, shall I ask Toby to extend my tenancy?' she asked. (Perhaps this wasn't the moment to tell Mrs B. she was working for Toby.)

'Yes please, once I've got rid of Mum's flat, I'm off!' was all she said.

Emma returned to her seat on the deck, it was now quite dark, but she sat quietly in the blackness absorbing the news. What with everything else that was going on, this was actually good news.

The good news didn't last long, seeing Melanie at the club a few days later, she joined her and got a progress report. 'There's a new service just being introduced,' Melanie told her. 'A car will bring you into a new area just alongside the terminal building, your hold bags are taken away and you wait in a lovely lounge, just like a four-star hotel. Then just twenty five minutes before your flight leaves you get called to a private scanner, with security staff just there for you. Then it's a minibus straight to the plane, and your bags are loaded last, so they should be first off at the other end.

On arrival at Miami, you'll be in transit, and there will be someone waiting for you, they'll get you through immigration in the fast lane and on to your next lounge. That will take you to Phoenix, it's another five and a half hours flying. It's not cheap, but it really will ensure you have a comfortable stress-free journey.'

Emma thought this sounded brilliant, 'And will it do the same on the return flight?' she asked. Melanie looked puzzled, 'You won't be flying anywhere, if you're going through the Panama Canal will you?'

'What? What did you say, the Panama Canal? No way, that wasn't the deal at all, I know nothing about this!'

Melanie flushed uncomfortably. 'Mr Brown called in at the office, he said he had decided to return via the Canal, it can drop you off when the cruise ship calls in at Bridgetown and you only need a taxi from there.

Emma looked skywards and said just three words. 'I'll kill him.'

'And I'll kill you if you laugh once more.' she told Toby when she got into the office next morning.
'This is grossly unfair, he hasn't even had the courtesy to discuss it with me.'
'That's because he knows you'll object' he told her. 'Look Emma, now he's got the idea of flying, getting a passport, leaving the country and jet-setting off, it's taken hold. He probably feels he might just as well get a cruise in whilst he's abroad. He obviously feels secure if you're with him and has decided to be killed for a sheep as a lamb.'
'Well, I'm the damned sheep,' said Emma, 'and I'm not going.'
'He has been very good to us Emma, we could never have moved without his help and support.'
'This is blackmail, and I won't stand for it.' was all she said.
Later that night she had a chat with Alan who was now on the point of flying back to the U.S. and learning the ropes.
'I think it's a great idea,' he said. 'It's probably the only holiday he will ever have off the island and all he's doing is choosing to return home by a different route, and it isn't as though you have to find the fare, what's your problem?'
Emma put down her mobile thinking the whole lot of them were against her. It rang almost immediately, it was Sandy ringing for a chat. 'A little bird tells me your going on a cruise, we need to talk about your clothes.' she said.
'And you, said Emma bitterly, 'are the last straw!'

CHAPTER TWENTY

Turning northwards next evening on leaving the office, she drove up to CB'S. If she was honest with herself she was resigned to the change of plan, but she certainly wasn't going to tell him that, and she wasn't going without a fight.

He was sitting in his usual place in the shade, he had a jug of iced gin and tonic in front of him and two glasses. 'Have you got company?' Emma asked as she joined him.

'Yes, you, I knew you would turn up eventually, if only to shout at me,' he said with a grin.

'And you would deserve it, you hadn't even the courtesy to ask me first!' Emma told him.

He had the grace to look slightly ashamed, 'I know, forgive me Emma, but I really would like to go and the Panama would be such an adventure, and anyway,' he suddenly regained all his old bluster, 'You owe me a favour and I can't go without you.'

Which was how one week later she came to be travelling to the airport with Charles Brown, their suitcases holding enough clothes to see them through the heat of Arizona and a cruise through the Panama Canal.

Melanie had been quite right, her expensive arrangements saw them escorted all the way and afforded every comfort. Charles Brown appeared totally relaxed, allowing himself to be shepherded through check in, security and all the other inconveniences associated with travelling by air. He sat gazing out of the window as the plane gained height and flew over familiar landmarks before banking and heading north west to Miami. He accepted drinks and snacks as though he was in one of his local restaurants at home, read his newspaper and watched the ground reappear with interest as they landed in Florida. Here they were met, escorted through immigration and settled in the VIP lounge, where they enjoyed a meal before boarding their flight to Arizona. 'Should have done this years ago, there's nothing to it.' he informed Emma, as they once again climbed into the sky.

Emma laughed. 'CB, there's nothing to it because you've paid the earth, we are travelling first class and every step has been arranged. Most people are crammed into economy behind us, they will have had to make all their own travel arrangements and will never get the chance to travel like this.'

CB simply grunted, but she was right, he thought. The advantage of never flying before today meant he could afford to do it in style. He simply looked sideways at her and grinned.

Once again they were met on arrival and whisked away in a waiting limousine, their bags collected and safely stored in its trunk. The thing that impressed CB the most, she told Toby, much later, was how the suitcases had found their way from Barbados to Miami, cleared customs and then were off again to Scottsdale.

The Receptionist at the Royal Palms hotel was waiting for them, greeting them by name and summoning the bellboy to show them their rooms. This was an eye opener, even for Emma. Melanie had reserved them a suite, they each had a bedroom and bathroom, but these were linked by an adjoining room. This comfortable lounge, had wifi, bar, fridge, writing desk, t.v. and every other conceivable luxury you could imagine, it meant they had the privacy of their own rooms but a mutual meeting ground. Privately Emma heaved a sigh of relief, she had worried they might have been allocated one room. She should have known better, Melanie needed a large thank you for all her arrangements.

The bellboy showed them around, demonstrating tv controls, air conditioner, shower settings, phone, teamaker, coffee machine and music system. When Emma complained she couldn't possibly remember all this, he grinned and said, 'Just pick up the phone, there will be someone to help you, anytime.'

That night they decided on room service. Even with every conceivable luxury along the way, it had been a long day and they were both shattered. The small uniformed staff had swept into the room, set up a small dining table with white starched linen, two comfy chairs, opened the wine and ensured the meal was perfectly served, before departing wishing them a good evening.

They kicked off their shoes, poured the wine and simply relaxed, both agreeing it was going to be an early night, they had an auction to attend in the morning.

Alan was waiting in reception next morning, throwing his arms around them both. He looked well, bronzed and happy. It was obvious he was absolutely loving the new job.

Emma hadn't really known what to expect, her only experience of auctions was to see cattle being sold on tv newsreels. This felt more like a theatre, with comfortable seating in rows, but instead of a stage they faced a track or road and Alan explained the cars would be driven slowly along this, so everyone had a chance to see them. The special cars would have been advertised extensively, with glossy photographs and details of mileage, condition and age. These weren't impulse buys, often the buyer had been looking for a particular model for years and was prepared to pay handsomely. They would have already paid a visit to the showrooms and examined their prospective purchase in great detail. Where big sums of money were involved, they had to be certain it was the right vehicle for them.

'There are representatives from a couple of the motor museums here,' he told them. 'So it could be an interesting outcome!'

Emma and CB sat and watched the cars trundle slowly past. Some didn't reach their reserve, some went for lower and others for higher prices than expected.

'Why are those folk on the phone?' CB asked Alan, who explained they may have been to see the cars in advance, and couldn't get to the auction, be out of the country or even wanting anonymity. They registered their interest in advance and simply bid by phone, the girls passing information on the bidding for them.

Then CB gripped Emma's hand. 'It's coming.' he hissed.

The car looked like something used for a state visit, its deep blue paintwork was polished until you could see your face in it, its white wall tyres spotless and the very size of it made everyone pause to watch its entry.

The auctioneer read out its provenance, only two owners, its low mileage and most importantly the care and conservation it had received for years and years. He began the bidding at one hundred thousand dollars, but warned the audience that he already had bids from overseas buyers. This was a very rare and desirable car he told them.

Afterwards Emma simply could not remember the next few minutes, the bidding went higher and higher until only two people remained, one in the hall, the other was a telephone bidder.

When the hammer finally went down, it was to the invisible buyer on the other end of the phone and CB was richer by almost two hundred and seventy five thousand dollars.

He and Emma had just looked at each other, they simply could not speak. She leaned forward and kissed his cheek. 'Congratulations.' was all she could say.

The silence was broken by Alan, who came to say they were invited to the directors offices for a congratulatory glass of champagne.

CHAPTER TWENTY ONE

'Oh, If it had only been one!' thought Emma, as she and CB were eventually off loaded outside their hotel. 'We shall have thick heads in the morning.' was her only comment as she gently guided CB towards his room, assisted with getting the key card the correct way up in the door and ensuring he was safely installed for the night.

Once back in her own room and kicking off her shoes, she went over the day in her mind. It really had happened, the car had gone, and CB was the richer for parting with something which had simply become an embarrassment. Wrapping herself in the hotel towelling robe and making a final cup of tea she felt a sense of déjà vu. The arrival of sudden riches, from an unexpected source reminded her of her mother's hidden hoard.

Alan drove them to Phoenix next day, the local flight would take them only eighty minutes, and he helped CB and Emma check in before they said their farewells. Emma laughed as he drove away, he couldn't wait to get back to his beloved old cars she said. The flight was cheap, cheerful and trouble free. Neither of them had been on anything so small, and they found the flight was both bumpy and very noisy.

'Don't know why they bothered to close the doors,' CB grumbled. 'You could see all the rooftops and gardens,' he complained, as they dragged their heavy cases from the carousel.

Their chauffeur was waiting, holding up the usual white card with their names printed in large letters, and they climbed into the big car, pleased to be looked after again.

'We're getting very spoiled,' Emma told him.

Both CB and Emma had seen the cruise liners in Barbados many times, but it wasn't until you actually stood looking up at their decks you realised how big they really were. Taking advice from Melanie they had avoided the 'floating cities' as she called them and were to travel with one of the luxury lines which carried only 450 passengers and had a crew of 390. Whilst most passengers were taking the full voyage from Los Angeles to Miami, others would be joining and leaving as the boat made its way down the west coast of Mexico on its way to the Canal. Once through, it would call at several of the Caribbean islands on its way north and Emma and CB would leave once it had berthed in Barbados.

Whilst passengers had hurried off the ship to board tour buses and taxis for their day in San Diego, Emma and CB did the opposite. Their luggage was unloaded from the car and after security clearance it was soon on its way onto the ship. They walked up the gangway, showed their newly acquired pass cards and were greeted warmly. The boat was quiet, most passengers having gone ashore, it would not leave until evening which gave them time to explore their surroundings. Once again, Melanie had proved her worth, they had a two bedroomed stateroom with Butler in attendance, the previous occupants having disembarked in San Diego. Ron their Butler, made them feel immediately at home, producing a tray of tea and coffee and explaining his job was to ensure they had everything they needed, just pick up the phone he said, which would immediately ring on his hip. Emma suddenly got the giggles, for one moment she had imagined his hip bone trilling loudly.

That afternoon they explored the ship after a late lunch, finding pools, library, cocktail bars, boutiques, cinema, a beautiful theatre and even its own hospital. They then sat out on their balcony admiring the stunning scenery around them and watching the passengers returning from their various excursions. Melanie had told her the new cruise ships could move just as easily sideways, as they did backwards or forwards and this enabled them to get moorings alongside the towns providing the water was deep enough.

'Should have done this years ago.' said CB, stretching his skinny legs and enjoying the moment.

Emma smiled, he was right of course, she really hadn't wanted to come, but the whole experience had been amazing, and now they were travelling home cocooned in utter luxury, it was fabulous and she told him so.

They arranged to meet later in the bar, Emma wanted a long hot shower and a hair wash. Looking at her fingernails she decided a manicure might be a good idea and picking up the phone, made a booking at the Spa for the following day. She grinned to herself, she had suddenly had a vision of her mother's face, a manicure! She would have been appalled at the sheer extravagance. However, it made her pause and realise how little she ever thought of her mother, just like Alan and Robert, their lives really had moved on.

She walked into the cocktail bar feeling much better, the slim fitting silk dress which Sandy had talked her into was just right for dinner on board. The room was crowded with passengers having pre-dinner drinks and she struggled for somewhere to sit. Then she saw a spare seat at a small table with just one occupant. She walked across and having checked it really was vacant, sat herself down to wait for CB who was late, Emma suspected he had gone to sleep.

Her table companion was a small, slim black woman, probably about sixty she thought, wearing a lovely two piece outfit. The skirt was a deep green satin, and the top was lace, but they were absolutely identical in colour. Emma thought it was one of the nicest outfits she had ever seen and impulsively told her so.

The woman gave her a smile, 'Thank you, it's a real confidence booster when you find you've got something right.' she said. Emma introduced herself explaining they had only joined the cruise that day, and the woman said her name was Millicent, but as everyone had called her Millie for the last thirty years, that was her name now. Soon they were chatting like old friends, she was travelling alone she told Emma, returning to Barbados after working for thirty years in Los Angeles. The cruise was part of her retirement package, and anyway, after thirty years she had so much luggage it would have filled the plane if she had flown home.

Emma liked her immediately, and was just starting to tell her about themselves when there was a disturbance in the doorway and a large, extremely overweight black man walked in. He had cut off jeans and a slightly dirty white tee shirt, seeing Millie, he stood legs apart, hands on hips and bellowed.

'You're here,' he roared, 'been looking all over the ship for you, come on, I've got some seats downstairs.'

The bar fell silent, Emma noticed Millie had gone grey at the sight of him, shrinking back in her seat.

'No, she whispered, 'No thank you, I am staying here.'

'Rubbish, he bellowed again, I've got seats downstairs waiting, now come on.'

Emma watched as the barman quietly picked up the phone, the rest of the room had fallen silent and simply stared, Millie simply continued to shake her head, she looked terrified.

Whatever connection he was to this woman, it was obvious she was frightened of him, and all Emma's protective instincts made her stand and address him.

'You heard the lady say no, I believe Security are on their way, I suggest you leave at once.'

'I've got us some seats,' he blustered, 'Been all over the place looking for her.'

'Well the lady has made it clear she doesn't want to join you, please leave, you're causing a scene.'

After that everything happened at once, two white uniforms appeared in the doorway and quietly took the man's arm. With very little resistance he was persuaded to leave with them, several men who had stood up ready to help, sat down again, the barman began pouring two glasses of champagne, placed them on a tray and brought it across to where Emma and Millie were seated.

'Drink this ladies,' he said quietly, 'You'll soon feel much better.'

And into this walked Charles Brown, who looked round in amazement at the two women sipping glasses of champagne and demanded to know what on earth was going on!

CHAPTER TWENTY TWO

Emma introduced Millie who was still shaken, the hand holding her glass trembled as she explained. He was no friend or relation, simply a man who had attached himself to her on the voyage and she had spent most of the journey trying hard to avoid him. She had become frightened when he refused to take no for an answer and had taken to hiding in places she felt he would not visit.

Emma excused herself and went to find the restaurant manager. She quickly explained the situation and organised their table to be changed to a threesome. Tomorrow she would see the purser and make sure Millie would not be bothered again.

Despite Millie's protest that she was not supposed to be eating in their restaurant, Emma assured her it had all been organised and the three of them enjoyed a late dinner. Charles ordered some more champagne, and as she relaxed Millie began to tell them about the years she had spent in Los Angeles.

Thirty years ago she had arrived at a beautiful house in the hills to find a scene of chaos. A family who simply needed help and organising. Gina, her mistress had been a small time actress when she had met Coln. He was in the film industry and did something complicated with cameras and films, she never did understand it, but most of it seemed to be animation and he worked hard and earned well.

In return he had expected Gina to run his home and their children smoothly, the house to be perfect and the meals beautifully cooked. When Millie walked into their lives, Gina was sitting sobbing at a piano, not playing, just sobbing. There were four children, the eldest was only five years old and she simply could not cope.

Millie had worked for them for three decades. She had seen 'her children' grow up, leave home, marry and begin to have children of their own. Coln and Gina's marriage had survived, mainly because she had made them see that people cannot be good at everything. Gina's skill was to be a charming hostess and look good, his to earn the money which would pay for the pool man, the gardener, the caterers and all the other tasks a large house needed. When school runs became part of their lives, they paid for her driving lessons and she spent part of her day chauffeuring children from school to tennis, to dance lessons, on to swimming and back for a bedtime story.

By this time she had staff of her own and cleaning and washing were simply supervised. Her job, Coln had said was to run the place from above!

Emma and CB were fascinated, this petite lady, who had never known who to expect when she answered the door had seen it all. Film stars, photographers, script writers, cameramen, directors and producers had all visited the house in the Los Angeles hills.

Millie explained that she had hit the big 60 this year, the children had all flown, the house was now too big and Coln and Gina were planning a cruise and a long tour of Europe. It was time to go.

She told Emma and CB, she had a little house in St Lucy, left to her by her parents and a niece who kept an eye on it.

'It hasn't been touched for fifteen years, so I know it will need work.' she told them.

By now they were just about the last in the restaurant and it was late. Emma excused herself, saying they had been up very early to catch their flight and she was going to bed. Charles said he was going to escort Millie to her cabin on the lower decks and ensure she was locked in, then he too would retire.

When he came back to their stateroom she was wrapped in her soft white bed robe and had made him a cup of English tea, which he had acquired a taste for.

'I have asked Millie to join us tomorrow, we're at sea all day.' He told Emma. 'You don't mind, do you?'

Emma looked at him and smiled. 'I can't think of anything nicer.'

Next morning she saw the purser and began to explain the situation. He stopped her politely. 'Miss Hird, security have already reported, the man has been warned. If he bothers the lady again he will simply be put ashore with his luggage. My company has a strict policy, troublesome passengers are taken off the ship, and they then have to find their own way home.'

As CB had company, Emma felt quite at liberty to indulge herself, she had a pedicure alongside her manicure, her hair was trimmed and she had a full body massage which left her simply wanting to curl up and sleep. 'Stay as long as you wish,' said the masseuse as she brought Emma a cup of fruit tea.

She didn't see CB again until dinner, he and Millie had enjoyed lunch, been to the cinema and then taken afternoon tea. 'Couldn't keep this up,' he told Emma. 'I'd be as fat as a pig.'

There was no further sign of Millie's tormentor and the next few days were spent sightseeing. They went to watch the divers in Acapulco and then spent time relaxing whilst the ship waited for permission to enter the Panama Canal.

They had loved Panama City with its new skyscrapers, and taking advice had ignored the tours offered by the cruise company and taken a taxi. The coaches were far too large for the narrow cobblestone streets of historic Old Panama, but their taxi took them down narrow alleys where the houses had been built to house all the labourers who built the Canal. Every few streets they came across a tiny church, where the men had worshipped, beautifully maintained and gleaming with candles and gold. The canal had made Panama rich from its tolls, and they had preserved their heritage, rescuing the lovely wrought iron balconies and houses in the nick of time. Now they were all preserved and painted pastel colours and together with the tour of the Presidential Palace, they agreed it had been a great day out.

CB bought himself a Panama hat, liked himself in it so much, he went back and bought a second. Emma and Millie stood and laughed as he admired his reflection in the mirror the old salesman held up for him.

They sat on the upper deck as they went through the Canal, this way they could see each side at once. Like many people

Emma had always imagined you simply sailed through with something coming the other way, and was astonished to discover this wasn't how it worked at all. Many of the modern ships had been built to take into account the size of the waterways. There had only inches to spare as they were pulled through the water by mules. Not the animals, the steward had said laughing, but little engines which ran alongside the locks and pulled the huge liner along. Soon they would finish building the much bigger canal at the side of this one, this would allow even larger vessels to avoid the long journey round the tip of South America. The first sets of locks took them into the huge Gatun lake where they waited for permission to proceed through the final sets and then once through these, they would be in the Caribbean Sea.

'Next stop Cartagena, Columbia,' Emma told them. 'Coffee, drugs or emeralds, which do you fancy?'

'Actually Millie and I thought we might do the tour, it visits a factory which shows how they cut the stones, emeralds I mean, not gallstones or rocks.'

Emma laughed, she wanted to see the Cathedral in the old town and the 16th century castle, she was perfectly happy to go off on her own.

When they berthed in Jamaica, Millie watched the man who had frightened her disembark. He staggered down the gangway with several other men, and the ship and her crew were delighted to see them go.

On their last evening they packed and made their final arrangements. They had watched the shows, seen the latest films, admired an art exhibition, attended a wine tasting evening and listened to an interesting lecture on the history of the Caribbean. They all agreed it had been a fabulous journey.

As they prepared to go down for the farewell dinner, CB produced a small box and simply said, 'this is for you.'

It was beautifully wrapped and tied with a tiny silk bow. Emma looked at him, puzzled, it wasn't her birthday or a special occasion.

'Go on, open it.' was all the old man said.

She slowly undid the bow and pulled off the gift wrap. Inside was a small square leather box with a hinged lid. Her fingers trembled as she pressed the catch and opened the lid. Then she caught her breath. Inside was a beautiful square cut emerald ring, round all four sides of the stone were narrow oblong diamonds. The effect was to encase the centre gem with a white surround, making the emerald stand out against the diamonds. It was stunning, the sort of gift a man would give his wife, perhaps just once in a lifetime.

Emma had never owned jewellery, there had been no one to buy her a bracelet or earrings for her eighteenth or twenty first birthdays. Her mother would have thought it outrageous and the brothers never had the money. Her only possession was her mothers gold wedding ring, and she could not bear to wear that.

'CB, I can't accept this, it's stunning, but you mustn't, I just cannot take it.'

The old man smiled at her, 'I knew you'd say that, but without you Emma, we wouldn't be here. I would never have flown, or cruised. Even more importantly, I would never have got a fortune for that car of mine. You and Toby, Bill, Sandy and Alan and ......' he stopped, suddenly choked, 'well perhaps you're all the kids I never had.'

She was crying now, the tears running down her cheeks, ruining the make up. This was the first time in her life someone had given her anything of such value.

He continued. 'I noticed you had no jewellery at all. That's unusual in a girl your age, so I thought it was time you had a piece. And anyway, it's out of the extra money we got for the car, so don't start saying you can't accept it.'

'Thank you, said Emma, 'you simply have no idea what this means.'

He stood looking at her, his head to one side enquiringly. 'No, I don't know your background, but I hope one day you will feel you can tell me.'

Emma nodded, 'Not tonight, we will have Millie wondering where we are, and my makeup is in ruins. But one day, I promise I shall tell you my story.'

CHAPTER TWENTY THREE

When Barbados came into view they were both awake and standing on their balconies watching the island growing larger as the Pilot boat guided them in. Emma experienced a strange emotion. Home. It really did feel she was coming home. No shabby house and cold rooms, no thin polyester bedding, no cheap food, bought because it was past its sell-by. She was sailing into a place she had grown to love and to friends who cared. She had almost forgotten how the girls in the office used to snigger at her out of date clothes and discuss their lively nights out on the town, while she said nothing.

Saying farewell to the crew who had looked after them so well, she heard CB promising them he would be back on board very soon. This time she thought he might have Millie for company. The two of them had got on so well. Millie's quiet good humour and calm was a good balance to his occasional grumpiness and lack of organisation. Emma thought they were made for each other, after thirty years of looking after other people she would have been lost with nothing to do, Charles Brown fitted the bill perfectly.

Despite all their protests, Bill Pearce was waiting for them as they docked. The trio stood and watched as several large trunks were unloaded, these contained thirty years of Millie's life and would have to go into storage. Then they were introduced to Millie's niece, who was a kindly woman in her forties. Millie was to stay with her until the house she had inherited was renovated. It would want a great deal of work she warned Millie, who evidently had not been home for a visit for several years. CB had already told her all about his tenant Bill, and his abilities as a local builder, and they arranged to meet up once she had settled in with her niece.

The house was spotless and welcoming. Winnie had put fresh flowers in the lounge, the windows shone and the little garden was immaculate. She and Lisamarie stood in the garden and clapped when Bill drew up and unloaded her cases, once again Emma felt the strange feeling of coming home, or was it love? Whatever the feeling was, it was a very new sensation.

She kissed CB on his weathered cheek, 'thank you for everything, I've loved every minute and we'll see you soon.'

'Come and have coffee.' was all he said, and climbed back into the car, but not before she had seen the emotion on his face. She wasn't the only one who had enjoyed every minute thought Emma.

With no jet lag to worry her, she was at work next day, surveying the pile of documents, forms, letters, files and everything else piled on her desk. This appears to be a new method of working, she told Toby. If in doubt, or unsure what to do with it, place it firmly in the middle of Emma Hird's desk. Toby nodded, and then ducked as she threw a file at him.

'First job is coffee, we need a catch-up before we begin.'

Toby ran through the cases which had been pending before she left, then went on to explain that a newspaper article exhorting people to make a will had given him a lightbulb moment. He had put an advert in the same paper, congratulating the newspaper on their article and offering to write a will free of charge providing they had their Conveyancing done at the same time, within two weeks business had doubled.

'So who has been doing the job while I've been away?' Emma asked.

Toby gestured, rather shamefacedly towards her desk. 'I've saved them for you.' He said.

Winnie came to the rescue. 'Just give me your washing and some coat hangers, once it's dry I'll do all the ironing, and you don't have to worry about a meal. I'll put a fresh salad and a cooked chicken in your fridge. This way, Winnie supplemented her income and Emma stayed at the office until late. Once the bulk of her paperwork was done she made the appointments with prospective buyers and sellers.

She had realised that to get enough details from them, even to write a very simple will meant each interview took twice as long, and if they were at work this often meant an evening appointment.

'Why am I doing this, I could be sat at home doing nothing.' she asked herself. Then answered her own question, 'Because it's a new practice, it's exciting, it's growing and I love it.'

Her email pinged just as she was finishing her salad. As promised Winnie had made her a platter of chicken salad and dressed it with herbs and a honey and mustard dressing, her favourite. Clearing away her plate she glanced at her email and saw it was from Robert, her brother.

That was unusual in itself, he was not good at keeping in touch and often went several weeks before she heard from him. It must be midnight in the UK, and Emma wondered what could be so important.

'Can you ring me when you have time,' he wrote. 'Alan says you should be back home by now and I would like to ask a favour.'

As it had just arrived in her mailbox Emma thought he must still be awake and rang his number. He answered immediately, so at least she hadn't got him out of bed, she thought.

After a great deal of small talk, how was she, how was the cruise, was she busy at work, he finally got around to the reason for his call. 'Do you think you could put me up in your spare room if I came over for a couple of weeks? I've more or less had the hard word at the office, business is quiet and I really should be using up my holiday allocation now, while things are slack.'

Emma was delighted, she had never imagined Robert would come over and visit.

'Of course you can come, it will be lovely to see you, I'm snowed under at work with being away so you may have to entertain yourself some of the time, but you can always borrow my car.'

'Could I come next week?' he asked hesitantly.

'There's a daily flight from both Heathrow and Gatwick, come when you want.' Emma told him, hiding her surprise.

'Well there's room on the BA next Monday, would that suit you?' he asked.

Emma said it would, she said her goodbyes and replaced the receiver feeling slightly puzzled.

Robert had already made enquiries, he knew which day he was coming and which airline. This wasn't like him at all, and she had a vague suspicion something was not quite right.

She was just considering washing her solitary plate when her phone rang for the second time, thinking it would be Robert with another question she was a second before she realised it was a completely different man's voice on the line.

'Have you fallen out with me?' The voice said.

It was Bill, she had promised to get in touch when he gave her a lift home from the docks, and she had completely lost track, that was almost a week ago.

Emma apologised, of course not, but she had come back to a pile of work. She had even been working evenings, seeing new clients and trying to catch up.

Bill laughed. 'Yes, I believe you. A certain person was boasting at the Club of his increase in business, he couldn't wait to show you when you got back.'

'Oh, he solved that problem,' Emma told him. 'He simply put everything on my desk!'

They arranged to meet the following evening at the office. Bill said he would be back in the yard by six and Emma promised she would work late until he arrived.

He was unlocking his big gates when she heard him, he drove his wagon into the yard whilst Killer came to greet her. The big Alsatian leaned on her, waiting to have his ears rubbed, and then he heard Bill moving his food bowl and promptly abandoned her for his evening meal.

Leaving the dog to his dinner, 'Come on, Bill called. 'We're both in our work clothes and I've had a heavy day, if you make the salad, I'm going to make a risotto, we can eat on my little balcony, drink cold beer and just chill. How about it?' Emma couldn't think of anything nicer, the thought of getting dressed up and having a late night did not appeal to her. Later as she drove home, having eaten Bill's risotto and drunk just one beer, she thought it had been one of the nicest relaxing evenings she had ever had, and what was more, she had a date, they had arranged to go up to a new restaurant on the west coast and have a meal.

CHAPTER TWENTY FOUR

Next morning was a Saturday, she had two early appointments, completed the transactions then rang CB and invited herself for coffee. To her surprise he had company already. Millie was sitting with him in the shade, their two heads bent together as they studied a pile of brochures.

'Millie, how lovely to see you.' Emma threw her arms around the tiny woman. Today Millie wore slim fitting cream cotton trousers and a bright blue silk shirt which suited her small frame.

CB waved a pile of car brochures at her. 'Come and help, Emma, we need a car for Millie, her American one was a left hand drive, so had to be left behind. She has to buy a new one, it's part of her retirement package. And I'm going to have one as well, can't be having taxis to St Lucy every five minutes, cost a fortune.'

Privately Emma thought you could have an awful lot of taxis for the price of a new car, but simply smiled and suggested they should go see the salesman who had found her a car when Alan had been here. As they had already given him some business she was sure he would give them a great deal if they bought two. What's more, we can ring Alan and check it out with him before we spend your money.'

CB thought this was a sensible idea. The two heads turned back to pouring over the glossy brochures and Emma went to the kitchen to beg a coffee. Daisy was making biscuits in the cool kitchen when Emma tapped at the door and went in. 'The two people out there are so engrossed in buying cars I have to find my own coffee, have you any to spare?'

Daisy was delighted to see her, she liked this clever intelligent girl who had absolutely no airs and graces and had changed her employers life. He had come back a new man, she told Emma, relating his flying and cruising experiences to everyone who would listen, as though he had been doing it for years.

'And it's not just the travelling,' Daisy continued, 'It's the lady, if she isn't here, he's away up in St.Lucy.'

'Do you mind?' Emma was suddenly aware this could have made things difficult for Daisy who had run this lovely house for fifteen years without any interference.

Daisy looked up surprised. 'Mind? Not at all Emma, I'm delighted. No one knows better than we do how lonely he was when his wife died, he threw himself into buying property, not for the money, but for something to do. Now he seems to have met someone who he might grow to care for, and she's lovely, keeps a low profile and has made it very clear she has retired from anything which might involve running a household.'

Emma breathed a sigh of relief, that had been a worry. CB was obviously so happy at meeting Millie, he might just have overlooked any future problems.

As she was leaving, Daisy said suddenly, 'He'll kill me if he finds it's me that's told on him, but did you know it's his birthday next Saturday? The big 7-0?'

Emma returned to the patio nursing her cup of coffee. The two car seekers were intending to spend the afternoon trawling the garages looking at cars. Poor Kingston, Daisy's husband, had been promoted to chauffeur and would be taking them.

Before they all left, Emma casually asked, 'Are you busy next Saturday night? I thought we might meet at the Club and have something to eat. We haven't all been together since Christmas, and you could bring all your photos.'

They all agreed this was a good idea, and Emma was left with the feeling that despite her current workload, her brother arriving on Monday and everything else going on, she was the one who would be doing the organising. The first task would be to ring round, let everyone know it was a birthday party and that it had to be kept a secret.

Fortunately Toby would sorted out the catering arrangements for her. He knew the Club's management much better than she did, and by swearing them to secrecy she was sure they would agree to pull all the stops out. A cake needed to be ordered, invitations would have to be made by phone and Sandy asked to come up with some fabulous table decorations.

With all these ideas buzzing in her head, she wished the pair well in their car search, and hurried home for a shower, a hair wash and managed to find time to paint her nails before Bill came to collect her. She had put on straight black silk trousers and a cream top which was trimmed with heavy lace at the hem and round the short sleeves. Bill regarded her with approval, 'You look good enough to eat,' was all he said.

They dined at one of the small restaurants on the west coast. It was busy with holiday makers, who favoured this part of the island, but it gave them a chance to catch up on all the events of the last three or four weeks.

Emma related the excitement of the car auction and the cruise home. CB, she warned him, had taken to flying and cruising as though he had been a veteran for years, they would never hear the end of it. At least now he had met Millie, she told him, he wouldn't be taking her off travelling again.

'Yes, said Bill, 'Toby was lost without you and I missed you too.'

For a moment she was struck dumb, but already the talk had turned to personal matters, and she realised Bill wanted to know more about her life.

In an attempt to divert his questions, she quickly asked, 'How about you, what made you come to Barbados and make a life here?'

Bill's face clouded, drawing a deep breath as though this was something he didn't normally talk about, he said. 'I was going to be married, Sara and I met at school, we kept in touch even when we were away at college and we had just put our savings into a small house on a new estate. Sara was out shopping, looking for bridal outfits, I suspect. Anyway, she didn't see the car until it was too late. It mounted the pavement, mowed down seven pedestrians, killing two of them. One of those was Sara. There was no court case, no revenge, just an inquest which found the driver had died at the wheel from a heart attack. He was dead before the car had even mounted the pavement.'

Emma looked at him, his face had gone bleak, this was a memory he hadn't spoken about for a long time.

Bill continued, looking into his glass of red wine and swirling the liquid round and round. 'I couldn't believe it, couldn't settle to anything, couldn't live in the house we had ordered, couldn't come to terms with the sheer bloody unfairness of it all. Mother didn't help, she had always expressed the opinion that I should wait, play the field and not settle for the first girlfriend. In the end my boss said I should take a break of several weeks, sort myself out and if I couldn't manage that, don't come back at all.

'So I came here for a holiday, got talking to someone who wanted a simple building job doing, and it snowballed from there. Small jobs to begin with, but I got recommended and it began to take off. CB had the yard behind the empty shop and suggested I could live upstairs over the shop and rent the yard for all my builders gear.'

He sat back, stretching his shoulders, it was almost as though it was a relief to bring the tragedy into the open. He continued, his mind on the past.

'I go back to see my mother occasionally, there has never been a father in my life, and she accepts my life is here. I've made a fresh start with no neighbours or painful reminders. As the years have gone on, I'm beginning to realise other things, and look at it objectively. Perhaps my mother had been right after all. Sara was a sweet mouse, there would have been no risk taking, no going self-employed, or flying off on an adventure. She was a stay at home girl, and the dreadful thing is, I've come to realise, eventually I would have been bored. I don't think I have every admitted that before, not even to myself.'

Emma held her breath, this explained why this good-looking man was here on his own, but now he was going to demand her life story.

She was saved by the waiter, who obviously wanted the table and suggested they had their coffee in comfort in the bar.

'Let's take a rain check, we've both had a busy day, and my brother arrives on Monday, so I've loads to do.' Emma suggested. That turned the conversation to Robert, and they talked about his visit and his work in London as they drove home. Any personal revelations on Emma's part, once again, delayed for the time being.

On Monday morning, Emma rang CB and asked if it would be ok to bring her brother to their Saturday meal, as he was arriving that day. 'Alan? Here?' He queried.

Emma laughed, 'no, afraid not CB, this is the other one, he's an architect.'

She rang off, reassured the old man had no idea they were planning a party, then rang Millie and let her into their scheme.

'Please keep it a secret, she told her, 'there are only a few of us, but we all owe him a lot in various ways.'

Millie promised faithfully she wouldn't breathe a word.

CHAPTER TWENTY FIVE

On Monday evening she stood outside Grantley Adams airport with a feeling of deja-vu, she had stood here several weeks ago waiting for Alan, now it was Robert's turn. I need a loyalty card, she thought. He came through, blinking in the unaccustomed heat, just as Alan had, and she moved forward to greet him.

'God Emma, Alan said you looked great, you're gorgeous, and you've shrunk!' was his greeting as he kissed her cheek. 'Is it always so warm at this time of night?'

Emma laughed, you'll soon get used to it, how was the flight?'

Robert grinned, 'didn't realise seven hours could go so fast, drinks, meals, films, reclining seats and a sleep, even a screen map showing where we are. Luxury, it was great.'

She drove him home through the warm darkness, and he sat quietly absorbing the sounds and smells. Emma realised she did not know this older brother as well as she did Alan. She had only been twelve years old when Robert had simply walked away at eighteen, his struggles to survive had meant working all hours and she had rarely seen him, he had never entered the house again until after her mothers death. She thought he took after their father, a quiet man who would put up with a great deal, but once a decision was made would stick to it tenaciously.

Robert wasn't hungry and by the time Emma had shown him around her little house, and he had unpacked his case, he admitted he was ready for bed. He had been up since 5.00am. in order to get to the airport, and the time difference meant he would probably be awake early, so he turned in.

Next morning she repeated the programme she had used with Alan and took him on her long walk to the beach. Just as Alan had, he gasped at the warmth of the water, having learnt to swim in the local canal, he had done it the hard way. That evening Emma took him to one of the little restaurants run by local

Bajans, and introduced him to blackened fish and rice, and the local beer. Once home, she poured two glasses of wine, sat him down on her tiny veranda and waited. She knew exactly what he would say and do, and he did not disappoint.

'The stars, Emma! I've never seen anything like it, they're beautiful, huge. You can see millions of them.'

Emma laughed. 'I sit here, just for half an hour most nights, never get tired of looking at them. Barbados is tropical, we're on a line with Africa here, and there is very little pollution. I just love it Robert, the warmth and friendliness, after ten years of mother'..... she suddenly choked and could say no more.

Robert nodded, 'I have a huge guilt trip because I left you and Alan to it, went off to follow my dream of being an Architect. Perhaps I should have stayed and helped more.'

Emma shook her head. 'No, you had the courage to go at eighteen, I still hadn't found the guts to leave at twenty-six. If mother hadn't died, I wonder if I would still be there, handing over my wage to keep that mausoleum of a place going.'

As he seemed to be in the right frame of mind to confide, Emma risked the question which she had been wanting to ask since he had arrived.

'What's wrong at home, Robert?'

He took a deep sigh, 'Nothing you could put your finger on, just a general discontent, my relationship with Lucy is over, she was the girl I brought to mother's funeral. It was good whilst it lasted, but we both wanted entirely different lifestyles and we are still friends, it was very amicable and we weren't living together which made it much easier.'

Emma thought he would stop there, but he continued.

'Work is difficult, we have always specialised in office building and design, the recession has hit us badly, no new offices are being built at the moment. We need to diversify into house building but the chairman won't hear of it. He has built office structures all his life and stubbornly refuses to accept that this problem could last for a long time. That's why we are all being pressured to take our holidays, the work just isn't there. Sooner or later he will have to make redundancies.'

It was probably the longest conversation she had ever had with Robert, and not wanting to break the spell she said. 'Couldn't you diversify, find another firm that builds houses instead?'

Robert laughed. 'That's where I become the problem, I don't want to design hundreds of identical houses for new estates, if I'm going to change jobs I want to design individual homes. The companies who do these are few and far between, and in this recession are not looking for new staff.'

Putting down his wine glass and getting to his feet he said. 'I'm to bed, enough of my problems, there is nothing that cannot wait. Thanks to mother I have the finances to do what I want, I suppose I could even take a year off and travel if I decided.'

On Wednesday morning she took Robert to see the new premises. CB had rung asking her to pick up some conveyancing documents and if she called tonight, he would get Daisy to put some refreshments on. Evidently Sandy was also calling in with some new sketches. She agreed but reminded him that her brother Robert would be with her. 'Send him up to Millie's with Bill, get him to earn his keep!' was all he said as he thumped down the phone.

She was in luck, when she went back inside she found they had pre-empted her. 'Bill has suggested I go up to see Millie's old place, he told Emma. 'Would you mind? He has a couple of other jobs to look at, and I might be useful.'

'Just as long as you're both back for 4.00pm at the latest, CB has called a meeting. He who pays the Piper, and all that…' she said laughing. Secretly she was delighted, it gave her another session in the office without feeling she was neglecting her brother. She watched as he climbed into Bill's wagon, after first being introduced to Killer, who grudgingly moved over so they had room for him.

When Toby heard she was going up to the Great House he begged a lift, his car was in for service and if Sandy was there he could get a lift home. CB got them mixing drinks, whilst he went out to greet Bill and Robert, who had just driven the wagon into the yard. Killer immediately rushed off to the kitchen, hoping

Daisy would have something tasty for him. Emma introduced Robert and they sat round the dining table waiting for Bill's report on Millie's place. There was a flipchart and notebooks and pencils set out.

'Saw this in a film on the cruise.' CB told them proudly.

Bill stood and explained that Chattel Houses had first appeared as homes for the slaves on the plantations. Many had been enlarged and improved, but they were always built to be moveable. It's a myth that wood doesn't last, he told them. If it was cared for and looked after it would last indefinitely. There are wooden buildings in Northern Europe which are a thousand years old. Unfortunately, this wasn't the case here, his best guess was that the old couple, Millie's grandparents had done little or no repairs in their old age, and her parents had followed the same pattern. Then when it was left empty and Millie was working in the States, it had deteriorated even further. The foundations were rotten, warmth and wet were a poor combination, rainwater had seeped in, together with rodents who had chewed their way through the place. Bill looked uncomfortable as he glanced at her.

'I'm sorry Millie, it is totally unrepairable, the only solution would be to pull it down and do a complete rebuild. As you know I had Robert with me, and he looked at the problem in an entirely different way. I'd like to hand over to him if that's OK?'

Emma looked at her, expecting her to be devastated, but she was her usual calm, serene self and simply nodded agreement.

Robert was obviously far more used to this style of meeting, Emma thought, as he walked to the front of the room and picked up the black marker pen.

'I know it appears bad news, but you're all looking at this as a simple repairs and renovations project. My job is to look at alternatives, and Millie' grandparents actually put their money into something far more valuable than the upkeep of one small Chattel house. They bought the land, probably very cheaply, and today it is worth so much more.'

Robert drew what looked like a slice of apple pie on the flip chart. 'The wide piece, it looks like the pie crust borders the road, this is on a feeder road to the main highway south. The land then rises, getting narrower as it climbs to the top of the hill, where there is a stunning view right across to the sea. All this land is yours Millie. You could build a fabulous detached house on top of the hill, three more nice houses on the way down, and more importantly a block of good quality apartments along the roadside. They could each have a dedicated parking space, a central entrance serviced by a concierge, air conditioning, fitted kitchens and walk in robes.'

'But who would buy them?' Millie asked.

Robert smiled, he had not spent a couple of hours on his laptop and years in architecture looking for likely building sites for nothing.

'Sixty six percent of the population of Barbados are between twenty-five and forty five. Tourism has given them good jobs. Hotel management, car hire, airport personnel, accountants, lawyers, chefs, food production, garages, estate agencies and many more. They all need somewhere to live and their aspirations are growing. They see the lovely big houses, the fabulous hotels, the good restaurants, and they want a part of it. A serviced apartment, with a built-in washing machine and dish washer in their kitchen, beautifully designed and decorated, this is all part of their aims. It won't be for families, it will attract the young career workers, and these apartments will appeal and sell to this growing section. And what's more, he finished before reseating himself, 'You could be involved in this project yourselves from start to finish.'

The room was silent whilst everyone absorbed this new idea, totally unexpected, it took some getting used to.

Only Millie appeared unmoved. 'Well,' she said, 'It's not the end of the world, I suspected the old place might be past saving, but I shall have to find somewhere else, I can't go on living at my niece's for ever.'

CB, expecting her to be upset and perhaps even tearful, had moved across to her side. Now he took her hand and said, 'Nonsense, you can come here, there is a perfectly good guest suite in the annex, it's got its own entrance and parking. What's more we have room in that big empty garage to store all your boxes and trunks. Don't even think of going anywhere else.'

Emma found herself suddenly choked and fighting tears. This lonely man had found someone he obviously adored and wanted to look after. The two of them were just so right together.

Daisy broke the spell by appearing in the room with a tray of canapes and a large jug of fruit punch. The act of passing glasses around, pouring drinks and generally helping, gave everyone a break to regroup their thoughts and examine their feelings about this news.

It was Bill who brokered everyone's thoughts. 'Building Project? What exactly did you have in mind?' he asked.

Robert shrugged, 'You have a builder, yourself, you could oversee the work and appoint the tradesmen, you have an interior designer who could design the apartments, you have a solicitor who could keep you straight. You have Emma whose conveyancing skills will go a long way towards pulling everything together and ensuring the bills are paid. If you need an architect, then I would like to apply for the job.' Before anyone could say a word, he continued speaking. 'There is a recession in the UK, I have no family or commitments there and little to go back to. If I got a couple of good references, do you think they might let me stay, for at least a year?'

Toby cleared his throat, 'Err, has anyone thought about finance, this will cost a fortune.'

'Not as much as you think,' Robert said. 'Millie owns the land, so we don't have to find the money for that. Toby can do the planning applications. We can build one, sell it, and build the next with the proceeds. What we need to do is to sit down and work out a ballpark figure for the first build.'

'No!' It was Emma who spoke. 'What we need to do is consult Millie. This is her land, and her old home, we don't ride rough shod over her feelings.'

'Millie, I'm so sorry.' Robert looked horrified. 'I saw such a great opportunity I simply got carried away, please accept my apologies, it was really thoughtless of me.'

To everyone's relief Millie simply laughed. 'I wouldn't have had a clue what to do with the land, and you are quite right, we need to sit down and talk about this in much more detail.'

By now it was after 7.00pm, and they were all hungry. Saying their goodbyes to CB and Millie, they stopped on the way home at one of the many Bajan eateries and had fish, black rice and beer. By unspoken agreement they did not mention the evening discussion. Walls have ears said Toby with a grin, as he and Sandy said goodnight and waved them off. Emma and Robert headed for home but not before he had agreed to meet Bill next day.

CHAPTER TWENTY SIX

The Saturday of the surprise Birthday Party had arrived much faster than Emma could imagine, but thanks to Sandy's efforts and Toby persuading the Club to put on a really good show, they were finally organised. They had asked Millie and CB to arrive at 8.00pm. The rest of them would be there at 7.30pm. giving them time to hide themselves and any presents, check out the final details, table settings and the chosen music.

They seated themselves in the Bar and when CB and Millie joined them they all appeared to be having their first drink and chatting casually. The head waiter arrived, announced their table was ready and they then deliberately took their time getting up and heading for the door, so that the birthday boy was first in the dining room.

The band had been primed and struck up 'Happy Birthday' as he entered and stood thunderstruck staring at the table in front of him. Each chair, dressed in turquoise and gold had a balloon attached to the back, the napkins, candles and vases were all in the same beautiful shade of blue. The tall vases held white lilies, roses and green and white foliage. The result was simply stunning.

'Who told you?' he asked, his voice choked with emotion.

Emma had been prepared for this question. She wasn't going to get Daisy into trouble.

'You're forgetting, I've seen your passport.' she said, fingers crossed at the small lie.

Once seated, he was astonished to see everyone dive under the big round table and come up with beautifully wrapped gifts, which they piled on the table in front of him. Thanks to Sandy, even the gift wrap matched the décor.

CB sat and stared at the intriguing pile, and looking at his face, Emma suddenly felt that, like herself, there had been times when there were no gifts, no surprises and no one who cared.

His fingers trembled as he unwrapped the first box, no mistaking it hid a bottle of something interesting. It was the finest rum from the Islands best makers, the bottle beautifully engraved with his name and the birthday date. The card said 'From Bill, and please can we have a taste sometime!'

Sandy had bought him a beautiful soft passport wallet, his initials engraved on the cover. He held it to his nose and smelt the lovely aroma of new leather. 'Now I shall have to travel again.' was all he said.

Toby, well aware how much he owed this man, had obtained a beautiful briefcase. One of Emma's conveyancing clients had told her of his trade in good leather items, and he had managed to find Toby one of the best briefcases he had ever seen. Both he and Emma had noticed his shabby old black document case and felt it was time he had a new one. He held it up, tried it for size and weighed it in his small hands, it was just right. 'You shouldn't,' he said, suddenly emotional again.

Millie gave him a kiss on the cheek and a small soft package. 'Huh, so you were in on this secret, and I thought you were on my side!' was all he said. Millie simply laughed. He opened her gift to find it was a pair of Vilbrequin swim shorts, bright pink and covered in grey octopus. Emma remembered him admiring them on other guests on the cruise, now he had a pair of his very own.

'I shall wear them on my next cruise,' he said proudly.

Emma gave him a small envelope which he opened and frowned. 'Driving lessons!' he exclaimed, obviously offended.

'Certainly not.' Emma said. 'It's an Advanced Driving Course for people who can already drive. They concentrate on refreshing your skills and introduce you to the latest technology. Very often the people who use this finish up showing the tutors how to handle a large or difficult car.'

Instantly reassured and mollified, CB thanked her and agreed it was a good idea.

Privately Emma had racked her brains to find a way to get him driving a modern car. He had only driven the old Cadillac for years and very infrequently at that.

It was a wonderful evening, reminding them of the Christmas they had enjoyed here. Good food, great wines, and a procession of people who came up to shake his hand and wish him a happy birthday. Balloons are such a giveaway! These included Frank Freeman who was dining with his wife at the other end of the great room and came to see what all the fuss was about.

'You old fox' he told CB,' shaking his hand, 'no idea it was your big 70, you kept that quiet!'

'I tried to, but they're very sneaky, did all this behind my back. Didn't know a thing about it. And whilst you're here can I introduce you to a new friend, Robert, he's an architect from London and I may need your help. He's Emma's brother.'

Frank instantly guessed what was coming. 'Get the paperwork done.' was all he said. He shook hands with Robert who had stood to greet him and with a wave to the rest of them returned to his own table.

Robert might be catching Friday's plane to Gatwick, but one thing was certain, he fully intended to return as soon as he had set his affairs in order.

Emma watching this exchange was intrigued, were they going ahead with this mad scheme after all? She pondered. Why else would CB have introduced Robert to Frank?

At the end of the meal, it was a very lively table who all insisted on a speech from the birthday boy. Champagne, good wine and coffee and liquors had all helped to relax them, no one would be driving and it would be nice to know they were forgiven for deceiving him.

CB stood and looked at them all, this was the family he and his late wife had so wanted, but it had simply never happened. Perhaps today the medical profession could have done more to help, but forty years ago it wasn't a possibility. Now at 70, He was suddenly surrounded by young energetic people who had skills and knowledge gained at Universities and Colleges he could never have imagined. He had helped them, but in return they had given him so much more, brought a lot of fun with them, and importantly more wealth, and best of all, Millie. She was going to be part of everything he had in the future, he was determined.

Clearing his throat, which seemed to have suddenly developed a choking sensation he began his thank you speech.

'This is not how I intended the day to run, no one was to know it was my birthday, you've all completely wrecked my day and I thank you, it's been a fabulous surprise and a lovely evening. The presents are just so thoughtful, although I shan't be wearing the Vilbrequins to walk down Bridge Street. Not just yet anyway, the legs aren't ready!'

Everyone cheered as he continued.

'All I intended to do today was to let you know we have made a decision on Millie's land. If I can rely on you all to put your own skills into this crazy idea, we will go for it. However we don't have to do it on an absolute shoestring, the money I got from the sale of the old car will be used to get us started. If anyone else has savings they would like to invest, then Toby must draw up a legal agreement which shows we all get the appropriate shares. We will need lots of planning meetings, loads of agreements and we're taking a risk, but I've always taken risks where property is concerned and this feels right. Emma, please schedule a date for our first meeting.'

With that the old man sat down with a thump. As it dawned on everyone that the madcap scheme was going to happen they began to clap, one by one they stood until the whole table was standing applauding him and clapping loudly.

CHAPTER TWENTY SEVEN

It was whilst unlocking the offices on Monday morning, she was puzzled to see Bill's wagon still in the yard as he was normally away long before she got to the office, then she saw him.

'I've been waiting for you Emma, I have to go back to England, my mother has died.'

He looked shocked, but not heartbroken. Emma made suitable noises and asked if there was anything she could do to help.

Bill had got the last seat on the evening flight to Gatwick, but if she could clear his fridge, take Killer up to CB's, let Joe know and take any phone calls he would appreciate it, he told her. He had let his current clients know, and thought he might be away two weeks, there was to be a post-mortem and her house would have to be cleared and sold, and there was no one else to help, he was an only child.

Making him a coffee and taking it upstairs, she knew just how it felt to face something so unexpected. It brought her own mother's death back into mind. Bill was throwing sweaters and Tee shirts into a small case. 'It's January, you'll need a coat.' she said.

'Haven't got one.' he said with a grin. Then suddenly serious he looked at her and said 'Emma, this is the end of my English connection, I already have Bajan nationality and will remain here, mother and I had a difficult relationship, can we talk about us when I get back?'

Emma gulped. 'Yes, there is so much about my family you don't know, never mind yours!'

With at least two weeks without Bill, Robert back home settling his affairs in the U.K., and CB spoiling Killer, she got her head down and ploughed through the backlog her trip had created.

Joe had been marvellous coming over on his days off to take Killer out for his long runs along the beach, much to Millie and CB's gratitude.

Millie had discovered he was saving every penny he could to buy himself some transport, and she and CB had decided they would make a contribution towards this, especially as he had his birthday coming up.

She heard the email ping as she arrived home two days later, it was Mrs Bristow, reminding her she would need her lovely house again. They were now in Panama City she wrote, and would be home in less than two weeks. Emma sat down suddenly, what with birthday parties, moving offices, trips and cruises, she had put this fact to the back of her mind. Now it was two weeks away and she would be homeless.

Talking it through with Toby next morning, he simply said, 'Go see CB. He has property all over the place, he's sure to have something.'

Which is how she came to be driving north at the end of the day having rung and invited herself for dinner and putting her problem to them both.

'I've been really late doing anything, after all I've known long enough, but it has suddenly caught up with me, anything at all will do, otherwise it's a tent on the beach.'

CB looked across at Millie who gave a slight nod. 'Come and live here, in the annex.' he said.

There is an en-suite in the main bedroom, guest room, house bathroom, lounge and a kitchenette.'

Emma was puzzled 'but I thought Millie was in there? I can't turn her out!'

The two people grinned, rather self-consciously.

'Well she was, but it didn't last long, she's now in the main house with me.'

Then regaining his old bluster, CB said. 'The trouble with you young people, you think anyone over fifty is past romance and all that.'

'I certainly do not, I think the two of you are made for each other. Millie has had thirty years experience of looking after difficult juveniles, and you have certainly been extremely lucky to have found her,' That made them all laugh.

Emma went on to say, 'If you don't charge a fair market rent, I'm not moving in.'

'If you don't pay the going rate, we won't let you!' CB felt happier now things had moved on from details of his and Millie's living arrangements. 'And I expect you to do my rental agreement free of charge,' he continued, with a grin.

'Consider it done.' she said with a smile. This was a far better solution than anything she had hoped for. Reasonably near the office, beautifully appointed, and private parking out of sight of the main house meant she could come and go without being under anyone else's nose.

Her move to CB's took two trips in order to fit in everything she seemed to have acquired over the last months. 'I arrived with a single suitcase, where's it all come from?' she asked Winnie, as they cleaned windows, changed beds and made the place absolutely spotless ready for Mrs Bristow's arrival.

'You flew in with your holiday clothes, Emma. Now you've got food, wine, more lovely clothes, an ipad, a printer, and more shoes than I've ever seen!' Winnie told her, as they packed all her extra possessions into cardboard boxes ready for the short journey.

Emma would miss Winnie, who had been such a great support when it came to keeping the place clean, making her a meal and taking the pressure off her when she was working late. She had arranged for a thankyou bouquet for Winnie and a welcome home one for Mrs Bristow, and fully intended to keep in touch.

Emma arrived at her new home to find an attractive olive-skinned girl waiting to greet her. 'I'm Fay,' she told Emma, as she helped unload the car and carry everything indoors. With an extra pair of hands, the task of putting everything in its place was a lot easier than Emma had expected, and she realised that since Millie had moved out to join CB, someone had spring cleaned throughout. There were brand new towels and bedding in the cupboards, new blinds at the windows, and a new fridge/freezer in the kitchen. Someone had given this place a makeover.

Fay smiled, 'Mr Brown said it needed a facelift if Miss Hird was moving in.' was all she said.

Once everything was in place, and Fay had left, Emma went to find Millie and to thank her for her thoughtfulness in organising some temporary help for the move. 'I just cannot believe how much I've accumulated, it took two car trips!' she said, as she kissed the smiling woman, who was seated in her usual place in the shade.

Millie laughed, 'Oh, she's not temporary, you'll be seeing much more of Fay. Daisy and her husband have looked after one elderly man for years and years. Now there are two of us to care for, plus you in the annex, and sooner or later, Robert will turn up. Just think of the visitors we have had over the last few weeks Emma. It's extra meals, refreshments, drinks, entertaining, and from what I gather we shall be having a great deal more business meetings about the building scheme. I've promised Daisy I will never interfere, but thirty years experience has taught me to recognise when extra help is required. Daisy loves her kitchen, her cooking and feeding us all. Fay will be here a couple of days a week, she will change beds, wash and iron, run the vac around and this way we avoid a build up of stress levels. It was Daisy who found her, she's come home from England after an unhappy love affair, has a small daughter and just wanted to be back home. She's been housekeeping at a London hotel, so knows all the ropes.'

Emma looked at the small woman, so utterly unlike her own late mother, 'Millie, she said quietly, 'you really are the best thing that has happened to all of us.'

As Emma was about to leave, a bright red 4x4 came rattling up the drive, it was CB obviously very pleased with himself, and anxious for her to admire his new vehicle.

'Well, they will certainly see you coming.' Emma said. 'That's just about the brightest red I have ever seen.' After this, she was treated to a tour of the car, CB demonstrating everything from the button that opened the huge boot, to the reclining seats which made the boot bigger still, to the sliding glass roof over his head, to the heated seats which had three different temperatures. 'You will definitely need those in Barbados,' she told him laughing at his delight.

With Millie's encouragement he had taken advantage of Emma's birthday gift and learned to drive an automatic, operate the sat.nav and use the reversing camera in the rear. Emma suspected he had spent most of the lessons telling the instructors all about the sale of his last car and his trip to sell it in the States, but after owning such a huge car for so long, he admitted he had found the smaller size and increased comfort amazing, and was driving at every opportunity.

'And that,' said Millie quietly to Emma, 'Is my problem.' She walked Emma round to the rear of the house and stood looking into the enormous garage, which had once held the old car. Inside was a small yellow Fiat, not new, but in good condition and looking extremely tiny in the huge space. The purchase of a car on her retirement had been part of her package, and she had chosen this small sensible vehicle, very suitable for the local narrow roads.

'I'm simply not using it,' she explained. 'If we go out anywhere Charles insists on driving me, and we go everywhere together. I know it was built into my retirement package, but I do wish I hadn't bought it, it is simply surplus to requirements! It's going to sit here for ever, just like the old Cadillac did.'

Emma looked at the car thoughtfully. 'You know, Joe is saving up frantically for some wheels, perhaps he might be interested, he's already having driving lessons.'

Millie brightened instantly, 'What a good idea Emma, now all I have to do is sell the plan to CB!'

CHAPTER TWENTY EIGHT

Meanwhile Bill kept her informed of his progress, his mother had simply had a heart attack whilst out shopping and the post-mortem had confirmed this and quickly released her body It had been a small funeral, just old friends and neighbours. He had cleared the house of furniture and prepared to put it on the market. His mother's only surviving sister was in a retirement home and had not attended the funeral, but he had been to visit her and acquired some interesting information! Emma looked at the exclamation mark at the end of his email, and was intrigued.

It took him three weeks, but in the end, taking advice from both Alan and Robert he had given the sale of the house to Alan's estate agent girlfriend. Anything in London was fetching a fortune, his mother had acquired the house just as he was born and it appeared to have been paid for years ago. It would fetch a good sum and give him the capital to join the St. Lucy Scheme as it was beginning to be known.

Standing once again at the airport, she felt she needed a loyalty card! But when Bill came through and simply put both arms around her she realised how good he felt about coming home. She drove him straight up to CB's, after her, he wanted nothing more than to see Killer. By the time she finally got both Bill and an ecstatic dog home it was so late, she simply waved and promised to catch up later.

It was three days later before they managed to get out for something to eat. Bill had spent some time pacifying clients, rescheduling jobs, responding to phone calls which had come in during his absence and thanking the friends who had helped out. Millie and CB got a beautiful bouquet of flowers and a bottle of his favourite rum, Joe received a healthy contribution towards his car fund and Emma was obviously being treated to a slap-up meal in the best restaurant on the island.

Sitting holding her hand Bill told her of the difficult relationship he had had with his mother, there had never been a father and he had never had his questions answered. Clearing the house he had found a photo in the bottom drawer of the dressing table. It showed a big man, his mother looking much younger and between them, a small boy he recognised as himself. The photo showed them standing outside a shop front. Looking closer Bill had realised it was a jewellers, and he had remembered it being in the High street for many years.

He had taken the photo and gone to see Clara, his mother's sister. She was frail and in a wheelchair, but her memory of things from the past was much sharper than today's events. She looked at the photo and smiled. 'Yes, its Ernie Swartz the Jeweller, we always thought he was your father, but she never did tell. You look like him.'

Clara went on to tell him his mother had worked for the Jeweller from leaving school. At first she simply cleaned and dusted the displays, learned how to polish and eventually became a useful shop assistant. Clara thought the relationship must have started then, she had always known her sister had someone, but not who. Ernie had taken her to jewellery sales in London and once to Paris, training her in the business he had said. The old lady remembered his wife, it had been her family who owned the business, any suggestion or possibility of a divorce would have seen him out on his ear and the end of a very good lifestyle. The pregnancy must have been a shock and there had never been any chance they would be together, but Clara thought he might have looked after his mother in other ways.

Clara was obviously tiring and Bill made arrangements to come again in a couple of days.

He had gone back to his old home and done some serious digging, he had also paid a visit to his mother's solicitor. As Bill had expected he was long gone, but his son, now about Bill's age saw him immediately.

Bill explained he was the sole inheritor of his mother's estate, he asked for and received the house deeds, they revealed that Ernie Swartz had purchased the house, and made it over into his mother's name.

'There is a note here in my father's handwriting' the solicitor said, 'it says Mr Swartz requested complete confidentiality and that the file should not be made available to anyone other than the lady concerned, but obviously her will, which is here with the deeds, leaves her entire estate to you. There are no bequests or legacies.'

Bill began to gather the papers together when the solicitor continued. 'There is also a small deed box in the strong room, I have arranged to have it brought up for you, but of course, it will be locked.

Bill produced a bunch of keys he had found in his mother room, some were tiny, obviously from old suitcases or boxes, but apart from a front and a back door key, there was only one likely candidate.

The small black tin box arrived, having been hastily dusted. The solicitor left him to open it in private. 'We never know what they contain, he explained. 'We once had an eccentric old lady who kept apples in hers.'

It certainly hadn't been apples, it contained a slim dark blue case and a small square box in red leather with a tiny gold clasp. He opened the blue case first, inside was a single row of beautiful pearls, graduated in size, the largest pearl the centrepiece. He knew nothing about jewellery, but he realised these were real and very good quality.

Turning to the second tiny box, it had to be a ring. He gently pushed the gold catch and it opened to reveal a single diamond solitaire, no fancy decoration, just one beautiful stone. It had a scrap of paper inside with the word Ghia written there.

Later he had Googled Ghia, and discovered they were the finest stones, this was a lovely ring, but to wear either piece of jewellery would have caused comment, people would have wanted to know where they came from, and what was a single mother doing wearing diamonds? So his mother had hidden them, she couldn't have the man who had given them to her and she couldn't wear his gifts, that would have given him away.

Emma had sat spellbound listening, so much of it was similar to her own story, the secrets, the deceptions, and the hidden wealth.

Bill continued his story, this explained several puzzles, although a single mother, he now realised they had never really been poor, his mother had taken a job at the cinema, first as the cloak room attendant, then as an usherette, finally becoming the manager. It had never dawned on him that the bills, summer holidays, school uniforms, and college fees hadn't come out of her cinema wages. Now he realised that would never have given them enough, money had been coming in from somewhere else. He hadn't had a father to teach him football or cricket like other boys, but someone had ensured he was always looked after.

'I assume Mr.Swartz is deceased?' he had asked as the solicitor came back into the room with two cups of coffee.

'Afraid so, many years ago, he was quite a bit older than your mother. But I think she kept him informed of your progress, my father handled his estate, and once said how proud he had been when you came out of college as Student of the Year.'

Bill looked at Emma and shrugged. 'So, I had a father I didn't know anything about, but who knew about me.'

Emma squeezed his hand, 'he gave you what he could. Today, with London house prices, you have come home with a wonderful inheritance, and you had a mother who was loyal to him, she never betrayed him, she must have loved him very much.'

They travelled home in silence in the warm dark, Bill simply drove them both home to his place. By the time he had let out Killer and saw him safely back inside, Emma had taken a quick shower, a deep breath, and deciding this was the most courageous thing she had ever done, had put herself into his bed.

'I should have told you before, this will be my first time, and I may not be very good at it. You see I haven't had any practice.'

Bill looked down at her laid in his bed, her chestnut bob and frightened face the only thing visible as she pulled the sheet up under her chin.

'Perhaps you should realise that I'm very out of practice, so there's two of us. Can we start with a cuddle?'

Toby, who wasn't always very quick on the uptake took some time to realise why Emma was wearing a slinky black dress which he felt was far more suitable for a night out, as opposed to the office. By lunchtime it suddenly dawned on him, she hadn't been home.

'I should keep a change of clothes in the office in future, it will over excite the clients if you look like that every day!' was all he said with a grin.

His own romance was finally going places. He had been in love with Sandy for years, but until he felt his practice was prospering and equal to hers he had not had the confidence to tell her. Now they could meet on level terms and the relationship was finally moving forward. Sandy had always fancied the six foot two man, who really should have been modelling, and she was quite content to let him think he was doing the running!

CHAPTER TWENTY NINE

The following Friday saw Emma boarding a flight across to Antigua. Bill had simply announced they were to have a weekend away on their own, and could she be ready mid afternoon? Could she!!!
'I'm getting used to trips and holidays.' She told herself.
The short flight and taxi ride meant they were settled in their hotel within sight of Nelson's boatyard in plenty of time for dinner. It was a beautiful setting, Bill told her that Admiral Nelson had simply copied his Portsmouth boatyard and built another like it in Antigua, so they had sail makers, officers quarters, boat repairs and everything they needed at both ends of their long journey.
They took a short boat ride across to a fabulous restaurant and had a lovely meal watching the sun disappear and the lights come on down in the harbour.
Perhaps it was the extra glass of champagne or the surroundings, but suddenly she found herself telling him the story she had hidden for almost a year.
With tears rolling down her cheeks, she found herself recounting the years, walking to save 10p, the cold house, poor bedding, second hand clothes and miserable food. The discovery of her dead mother and her deceit, the hidden wealth, and how the realisation that their sacrifices had been totally unnecessary had made them all feel very bitter and unforgiving.
It had been the release she needed, once someone else knew, it felt she had nothing more to hide and Emma experienced a feeling of lightness. As though a weight had been removed from inside her, it no longer mattered, she realised, it was over.
Bill had simply held her close, he had never experienced her poverty, but could understand better than anyone that parents could be devious and secretive, sometimes for years and years.

They sailed, swam, made love and ate good food. More than all those things, they talked and talked. Coming back late on

Monday evening they both felt that something which had begun as an attraction had turned into something very permanent.

Next day she kept her promise to CB and Millie. Inviting herself to join their evening drink and sitting outside in the warm dark, nursing a glass of good wine she told them her story. This time there were no tears, she simply told them of her fathers' departure, of Roberts determination to become an architect and of Alan's escape. She told of her ten years of poverty, supporting a supposedly destitute mother, her lost job, her mother's death and the desire for a long holiday somewhere warm. She was surprised to find how much they already knew, both brothers having revealed different bits of the story.

Millie and CB had simply held her close and expressed their feelings. Friendship, honesty and right now their love, were far more important than the past. 'We have all known poverty at different times in our lives, but it makes us appreciate the good things, so much more.' Millie had said.

With CB's agreement, Millie had sold her little yellow Fiat to Joe. With his wages from the office move and the Club, his birthday money and the cash he had earned from looking after Killer, he had completed his driving lessons and passed his test first time. Now he was the proud owner of the little car which he kept in immaculate condition. CB said he spent more time polishing it, than driving, but as Joe always reminded them, this was his OCD!

Coming home two weeks later she paused as she unlocked the door to the annex, and listened. Someone was talking, and although she was unable to hear what was being said, the timbre of the voice was familiar. Dropping her briefcase and bag in the hall, she walked round to the Great House and stared in amazement. Robert was sitting there, a beer in his hand and talking to CB and Millie , telling them of his journey back to Barbados.

'How on earth….why didn't you let me know you were coming?' She said, as he rose to give her a hug.

'Your fault, Sis' he said. 'I've tried the house but there was no reply and I'd got a standby seat on today's flight. In the end I rang CB and he said to jump in a taxi and come here. You didn't tell me you'd moved in.'

Later, Robert explained he had rented his nice flat out, with the help of good references which Alan's girlfriend had obtained, the agreement had gone through quickly as the new tenant was a Solicitor, and suddenly he was free to leave. The flight had been full, but by turning up and hoping for a seat he had only time to make a quick call before boarding. Once in Barbados he had rung CB when he couldn't get hold of Emma.

'I'll find a hotel, don't worry.' He told her.

'Nonsense, if Emma can put up with you in her spare room, you can join the madhouse here!' It was CB, who was delighted to have his Architect back. With that, he put down his beer and invited Robert to come and inspect his new car and the two men wandered off.

Millie looked at Emma and smiled quietly, 'Now you can see why we need Fay, CB is simply loving all the comings and goings. Any minute now Joe will come tearing up, Bill will bring Killer, Sandy is due with some sketches for one of CB's houses she's in the process of modernising, and they all need feeding, and he's loving every minute of it.'

Millie described the next few weeks as 'settling in'. They were all aware Emma and Bill had become a serious item, she often stayed over at his place over the office and everyone was delighted with their obvious happiness.

Air Cargo had rung Robert, and he had taken delivery of a large packing case which arrived from England. This contained his drawing board, a worn and comfy high stool, his tools and a large portfolio of drawings of houses and apartments he seemed to have acquired from somewhere.

Emma looked on in horror, 'Where are we going to put these?' she asked him.

Robert laughed, it had all been arranged he assured her. When CB had been showing off his new car it had struck them both that they were only using one fifth of the garages' huge capacity. If we had some windows in this place, you could use it as your office, he had told Robert. That meant Bill was involved in the alterations and two new picture windows were going in, together with retractable outside blinds to help with the glare. Robert could now work in peace, and he was on site when CB took him off to look at his properties, land sales and future plans and possibilities. He had bought himself a smart sports car and the two of them were simply having a ball, Millie had said.

CHAPTER THIRTY

She was sitting on the new wooden bench which Robert had placed at the top of the escarpment, the beach and ocean spread out below. He claimed that this spot at the end of the huge garage was one of the best views on the island, far too good for a garage, it should have a lovely house on it. The beautifully carved bench had been a belated birthday gift, a thank you he had told CB for making the three siblings so welcome, and for making the different generations feel like a real family. Emma guessed that even Robert had not considered that this had worked both ways, and they in turn had given the elderly childless couple a family as well.

She watched the distant figures of a tall couple who were walking along the waters edge, the small child with them was running excitedly in and out of the shallows, and she suddenly realised it was Robert and the woman with him was Fay. Millie had said something about Fay and an unhappy love affair, but that was all. Now it appeared she had a small child as well. As she watched them, she saw Robert swing the child up in the air and onto his shoulders, she smiled to herself, this explained his absences on an evening, she thought.

As she sat watching the sun going down, thinking of how far she had come in one year, a pair of hands circled her from behind and Bill kissed the top of her head and came round to join her on the bench.

'Penny for them.' he said, realising she had been miles away.

Emma smiled. 'It's a year today since I found my mother on the kitchen floor, I was simply marvelling at how things have changed. I love it here, I have a job I adore, great friends, and want to make this my home.' she told him.

Emma knew the day to day poverty and routine she had endured would always be there in her memory, but it made her appreciate what she now had all the more. If you had always had wealth, you took it for granted, but she would always enjoy the feelings of security and comfort she now had.

Bill smiled quietly, 'I've been meaning to do this for days.' he said. 'I already have Bajan nationality, and once we are married you will automatically become a citizen. I wondered if you would like to wear this?'

He held out the small red leather box she had seen once before, the beautiful diamond solitaire which had never been worn, but was of the very best quality that money could buy.

'It deserves to be worn, it's finer than anything I could afford, and I would love to see it on you.

Like you Emma, my life is here, but I want to share it with you, there is so much we can do.'

Looking up at him, her eyes brimming with tears, she simply said 'Yes, please'

The rest of the evening was spent in the crook of his arm, congratulations came from all sides. Daisy produced champagne and Emma had rung Alan with her news. Sandy arrived just as Robert came in from his beach walk, and it was hugs and celebrations all round.

Later Bill said rather hesitantly, 'How would you feel if I organised our wedding? It needs to be fairly soon owing to your visa, and I have a couple of ideas. If you worry about the dress, can I do the rest?'

Emma looked at him in amazement, then thought, 'Why not?' She herself had no experience of weddings, had never been closely involved in one and although she had given it very little thought, she expected they would have a quiet ceremony with a few close friends, neither of them were religious and she certainly didn't want a big church do. She was also absolutely sure that Sandy would be involved somewhere along the line.

'Well, if you're sure, I really hadn't thought about it to be honest.'

Bill smiled, 'Go find your outfit, let me do the rest, I've been thinking about it.'

Which is how, once again she came to be on a flight to Miami, seated next to Sandy, who had cleverly combined her usual winter trip with their shopping expedition. As they flew over the ocean the girls poured over the bridal magazines they had brought with them, exchanging ideas and opinions.

Emma insisted she would not look like a white puff ball, at her age she thought it quite unsuitable. Sandy had laughed, they were out of fashion anyway, she told Emma. They would be looking for something sleek and straight, preferably in cream, she assured the nervous bride.

It was a fabulous four days, Sandy appeared to have very few clients and they spent a great deal of time searching for just the right outfit. By evening they both kicked off their shoes and collapsed into two comfy restaurant chairs, but each day had brought exciting discoveries and they both felt that their purchases were just right.

Sandy, who Emma had appointed bridesmaid, had found herself a dress of the palest of pink silk, it had fitted perfectly and the colour was perfect against her dark skin.

Emma kept having to pinch herself, she was the owner of a beautiful cream full length dress. A wedding dress! Hers! It was the colour of Jersey Milk, its fine fabric pleated and tucked around her bust and shoulders and then falling into a lovely full length skirt. Once she had stood looking at herself in the shop mirror, she had met Sandy's eyes, and the two girls had simply nodded. This was the one.

Back in Barbados, she had taken the huge dress bag across to the Great House, where Millie had promised not only to hide it, but to hang it out and guard it with her life.

She had expected the Christmas arrangements to follow the routine of the previous year, when they would all meet on Christmas Day and enjoy the facilities of the Club, so was surprised when Bill informed her that they were to spend a quiet Christmas Day with dinner at CB's.

Why? she had queried. Have we fallen out with the Club?'

Bill grinned, 'We have a busy Boxing Day, we get married at the Club, it's all arranged.'

Emma sat stunned, this explained the whispers, the mysterious phone calls, the conversations that ceased when she appeared. She slowly absorbed the news, realising that it was a perfect venue, full of people and staff they knew, licensed for weddings and it would give them a wonderful reception after the ceremony.

She wasn't really sure she liked surprises, there had never been any nice ones with mother.

'And that, said Bill, 'is all you need to know at the moment, I still have a lot of arrangements in hand.'

'Hang on a minute, there are things I do need to be involved in, for example who will give me away? I accept your keeping secrets, but I need to have a say in somethings. Neither of us have any parents or near relatives coming.'

Bill just smiled. 'Well, I assumed CB would be asked to do the honours, was I wrong.'

'No, you're not wrong, I just needed to know' she said.

'Well, go ask him, that's one job you're allowed to do.' He said laughing at her.

Finding him sitting with Millie in their usual place in the shade, she had addressed the pair of them.

'I'm sure you're both up to your necks in all this undercover planning, but there is one thing I need to know. CB will you give me away, please?'

The old man looked at her and seemed to have something caught in his throat, he simply nodded until Millie squeezed his hand, and gave him time to recover himself.

'I've never given anyone away before.' He said rather slowly.

'Well, I've never been married before,' said Emma, 'So between the two of us we have to get this right!'

CHAPTER THIRTY ONE

Sitting in the office, supposedly working on a conveyance, she found herself staring into space.

Who was going to organise table settings, invitations, flowers, colour schemes, speeches? Would they remember to ask Winnie and Joe's Mum? The questions just poured out of her, she really wasn't sure she liked surprises. Then she steadied and reassured herself, Sandy would be there and her arrangements would be superb as always. She knew what colour the dresses were and would work around that. Stop worrying, she told herself, just enjoy.

Bill had said he was staying down at the yard Christmas Eve, he had several things to do before he came up to join them for Christmas Dinner. On Christmas morning Emma dressed and went across to the Great House to offer her help setting the table or give a hand in the kitchen. She found Fay already there, together with Lily her daughter.

The lovely old mahogany table had always seated them comfortably, but today someone had inserted extra pieces and it looked enormous. Millie was just finishing laying out scarlet napkins and smiled as Emma stared. 'I thought we were having a quiet day, how many are you expecting?' she asked.

Millie shrugged, 'Well you never know just how many to expect at Christmas, do you?' she said serenely.

Emma was still trying to add up the numbers when Daisy summoned her, the best china was in the tallest cupboards, could Emma please come and get them down, no one else could reach.

She was just asking Millie how much cutlery they needed when Sandy and Toby came in. Both were wearing a set of reindeer antlers on their heads, and Sandy's were trimmed with flashing lights, there was a battery hidden somewhere. CB shook his head, 'It's just like having children' he muttered, Only you're all several sizes larger.'

They were still laughing when she heard Bill's car, and what sounded like several pairs of feet at the door. Emma stared in disbelief as Bill came in followed by Alan and a small red haired girl.

'Happy Christmas sis! Meet Julie my tenant in London, we're here for the nuptials.' Alan said, giving her a kiss.

Later when everyone had a glass in their hands and things had calmed down they explained. Julie and he had kept in touch and they had managed to meet up when Alan had been across to the UK on car searches. The plan had been to spend the Christmas holidays in San Diego, but once Bill had contacted them, and told of the wedding, this had been changed to Barbados. They were staying at the Hilton and Bill had picked them up from the airport the previous day. Julie had saved up her holiday entitlement, this was her summer holiday, but in December.

'We're taking things slowly,' Alan told Emma, when she finally got a few quiet moments with her brother. 'I know we could have stayed with you or CB, but we need time to get to know each other first. So we're at the Hilton, we're having a beach holiday and it's great.'

Emma had never seen him look so happy, he glowed. She squeezed his hand and told him how pleased she was.

'We've all waited an awful long time to experience real happiness.' she said.

It seemed ridiculous to have turkey and all its trimmings in the heat, but somehow it had worked.

The house smelled of cooking, pine needles, canapes, punch and good wines. Millie's years in Los Angeles had given entertaining here a fresh look on the traditional Christmas dinner.

Daisy and her husband, Fay and her small daughter, all joined them for the meal, this explained all the place settings, thought Emma. The starter was a beautiful pale green gazpacho, Emma hid a smile, a year ago she would not have known you could actually have cold soup.

Only the Turkey and all its trimmings was a nod to tradition, and Daisy had avoided the heaviness of roast potatoes, sprouts, and stuffings. There were small squares of sweet potato, tiny sausages, a jus of cranberries and small bright green peas giving the dish a pop of colour.

It was too warm to consider Christmas pudding, so they had settled for salted caramel ice cream with a splash of Amaretto instead, a strange combination which surprisingly worked wonderfully.

Afterwards they took their coffee outside, sitting on Robert's bench watching the sunset. Julie expressing utter amazement at the wonderful display of colours and cloud formations.

Everyone left early, tomorrow would be a busy day. Bill took Alan and Julie back to the Hilton and went home to finish his speech, he informed them. Toby had said he would help Sandy with the decorations and flowers and the two of them went off to the Club.

Daisy and Fay washed up and Robert used his height to put away the great dinner service, which obviously only came out on very rare occasions.

CHAPTER THIRTY TWO

Her first thought on waking was. 'It really is my wedding day.'

So often as a dreamy teenager she had absorbed the romantic novels and real-life love stories from magazines and paperbacks. By the time she had reached her middle twenties, she had grimly realised that as far as her life was concerned, it was never going to happen. Mother had seen to that, with feigned illnesses and fevers if ever it appeared Emma had even a remotely potential suiter, she would take to her bed and declare she was too ill to be left alone.

Today she would be the bride, and she still found it impossible to believe. The arrival of the hairdresser and make up girl, one of Sandy's recommendations, had dispelled that idea.

By the time her hair, nails and face were done, Sandy arrived having spent the morning putting the last minute touches to the arrangements.

Millie helped her into the beautiful cream dress, whilst Sandy took a very quick shower and then slipped into her own bridesmaid outfit.

She was standing looking at herself in the long mirror when Robert put his head around the door. His eyes widened when he saw her, 'Sis, you look absolutely beautiful', he said. His voice was choked and like her, he was remembering the past. Clearing his throat he said, 'I'm to take Daisy, Fay and Millie in my car.'

'You've got a sports car!' said Emma, puzzled.

Robert grinned, 'I've got the holy grail, CB has lent me his precious red 4x4, on condition I drive it very carefully.'

Once they had left for the Club, and the pressure of all the preparations was behind them, the house seemed to settle. She and Sandy were ready and now only Daisy's husband remained. He would lock up and drive them together with CB to the club in the lovely limousine, hired just for that purpose.

Fay had brought in a tray of champagne, the last task before they had left for the Club with Robert,

And Emma poured a glass for herself and for Sandy.

'Thank you for your wonderful friendship.' she told her.

Sandy laughed, 'You never know Emma, one day you might do the same for me!'

CB arrived, looking immaculate in the beautiful cream dinner jacket he had bought on the cruise.

'I'll have one of those as well.' he said, nodding at the champagne. 'My nerves are all over the place. I don't have to do a Father of the Bride speech, do I?'

'Of course you do!' both girls said at once, and laughed at his horrified expression.

As the car slowly came to a halt at the Club, Emma gazed in amazement. The beautiful manicured lawns to the front had been transformed, there were at least sixty gilt chairs set out, each decorated with a cream bow. They faced a small gazebo with a stage surrounded by beautiful cream and pink flowers, plants, foliage and ribbons.

Almost every chair seemed to be occupied. She could see friends from her stay in the hotel, her neighbours, Winnie and Lisamarie, Mrs Bristow her old landlady. There were conveyancing clients, friends from the gym, Joe's mother and her friend. Frank Freeman and his wife were there. She recognised friends of Bill's from the building trade. His suppliers and tradesmen, people he had worked with for years. Someone had been very busy indeed.

Alan and Julie were seated in the front row, together with Fay and Robert and the small bridesmaid, it was Fay's daughter, Lily, carrying an old fashioned horseshoe and dressed in the identical pink of Sandy's dress. She could see Millie and Daisy, both waiting for the bride's arrival and their menfolk to join them.

Waiting for her on the small stage was Bill and his best man Toby, together with a tall slim black man in a long white surplice. This was the Canon who would marry them.

And because Emma had said she did not want to walk down the aisle in silence, at the side of the stage was a small trio, a steel band playing softly to the guests.

Joe was waiting for her, looking extremely smart in his new cream jacket.

'I'm the Master of Ceremonies today, he told her, as he helped her out of the car. 'I've been practicing all week with Alex's help.'

'Wish I'd had some practice.' CB said grumpily, he looked a strange shade of almost green.

'You'll be fine, said Emma, 'All you have to do is walk slowly, and anyway, I'm the one that should be nervous, not you.'

But she thought, I'm not nervous. Excited, yes, but it feels just right.

With a signal from Joe, the guests stood, the music changed to 'Yellow Bird' one of her favourite Caribbean tunes and she took CB's arm. 'Ready?' she asked.

The elderly man simply nodded, he was beyond words, and they walked slowly across the grass, down the centre of the waiting guests and climbed the two steps onto the stage. Once there he took his place alongside Sandy as witnesses to this special occasion and Bill smiling, walked forward and took her hand in his.

One day he would create and build them a house, he said Robert would be there to design it. They would be part of the scheme to build on Millie's land, CB had begun muttering about needing a bungalow, Sandy wanted somewhere her potential clients could come and discuss their requirements, a show room to display her ideas and skills.

The ideas had simply tumbled out of them, 'We'll take everything as it comes,' he had told her.

But today, whatever happened, could never be surpassed, she was a bride, in a beautiful dress, marrying the man she loved, surrounded by friends, and her heart felt as though it would burst.

TYPHOO LAGOON 70
~~BEACH~~ ~~GODS~~
P/APPLE   6
MEAT/STEAK.   23
             ———
              89

95 DOLLARS

Printed in Great Britain
by Amazon

20595895R00089